Instant stardom

It was w   we were go   all we could do was pick up speed and hope that our seat belts worked.

The Bikini Dust show was everything Dean had hoped it would be. We soared that night. All those tedious, painful rehearsals had been worth it.

As I stepped up to the mic in the white minidress that my mum had got married in (and which Jane would later spill lager on) and said, "We're The Hormones and we've come to steal your souls," there was an audible hum in the room. It got louder and louder as we blazed our way through the set, and then exploded into clapping and cheering and people going, "Woo woo!"

When Tara and I tried to get to the bar after we came off stage, we found we couldn't walk more than two paces without getting pounced on by record company types.... When we did eventually make it to the bar, we found Dean deep in conversation with this ridiculously handsome, twenty-something guy in a sharp suit.

"This is Paul," Dean said. "He wants to manage us."

And with those eight words everything changed.

OTHER SPEAK BOOKS

GUITAR GIRL

sarra manning

Naperville Central High School
LRC

speak

An Imprint of Penguin Group (USA) Inc.

SPEAK

Published by the Penguin Group

Penguin Group (USA) Inc., 345 Hudson Street, New York, New York 10014, U.S.A.
Penguin Group (Canada), 10 Alcorn Avenue, Toronto, Ontario, Canada M4V 3B2
(a division of Pearson Penguin Canada Inc.)
Penguin Books Ltd, 80 Strand, London WC2R 0RL, England
Penguin Ireland, 25 St Stephen's Green, Dublin 2, Ireland
(a division of Penguin Books Ltd)
Penguin Group (Australia), 250 Camberwell Road, Camberwell,
Victoria 3124, Australia (a division of Pearson Australia Group Pty Ltd)
Penguin Books India Pvt Ltd, 11 Community Centre,
Panchsheel Park, New Delhi - 110 017, India
Penguin Group (NZ), Cnr Airborne and Rosedale Roads, Albany,
Auckland, New Zealand (a division of Pearson New Zealand Ltd)
Penguin Books (South Africa) (Pty) Ltd, 24 Sturdee Avenue,
Rosebank, Johannesburg 2196, South Africa

Registered Offices: Penguin Books Ltd, 80 Strand, London WC2R 0RL, England

First published in Great Britain by Hodder Children's Books, London, 2003
First published in the United States of America by Dutton Children's Books,
a division of Penguin Young Readers Group, 2004
Published by Speak, an imprint of Penguin Group (USA) Inc., 2005

1 3 5 7 9 10 8 6 4 2

THE LIBRARY OF CONGRESS HAS CATALOGED THE DUTTON EDITION
UNDER CARD NUMBER: 2004299584

Speak ISBN 0-14-240318-0

Printed in the United States of America

Just as Molly was inspired by Ruby X, I was inspired by these ladies: Patti Smith, Sleater-Kinney, Kristin Hersh, Kenickie, Ronnie Spector, Etta James, The Donnas, Tanya Donnelly, Bessie Smith, Courtney Love, Hope Sandoval, Liz Phair, Missy Elliott, Dusty Springfield, Kylie Minogue, Darlene Love, Beyoncé Knowles, Laura Nyro, Le Tigre, Nancy Sinatra, Madonna, Ella Fitzgerald, Eve, Garnetta Deeds, Sarah Cracknell, Nina Simone, and Kim Deal.

Thank you for the songs that changed my world. This book wouldn't have existed if it hadn't been for you.

—Sarra Manning

GUITAR GIRL

There's a stack of folders piled up on the desk in front of me. All neatly labeled and indexed. A file for every month that I was in The Hormones. It's weird to see a year of your life measured out in press cuttings; legal documents; and receipts from restaurants, hotels, and musical-instrument shops.

I reach blindly for the folder nearest to me, and a photograph falls out. There's the five of us staring out arrogantly because smiling in photos was uncool. My hair was cherry red then. I look much younger. I'm wearing jeans and a green halter-neck top, a pink flower pinned in my hair. Flowers used to be my trademark, my thing. When we did gigs, fans would throw flower petals at me. Once in Birmingham, as I was walking offstage I skidded on a big wet clump of petal mulch and slid right into the audience. Dean had to run to the lip of the stage and haul me out, while Jane nearly peed herself laughing.

I look back at the photo. Jane's standing next to me, an arm slung nonchalantly around my shoulders. She's all hipbones and platinum blond attitude, a diamond navel piercing glints in the light from the ring flash. I remember how she'd tugged down the waistband of her black trousers in between shots. "You've got to show a bit of flesh," she said, laughing when I pointed out that you could see her knickers.

Then there's Tara, slightly to the edge of the shot. Short, spiky hair that Jane had bullied her into dyeing black, and a bright red bra visible through the thin white cotton of her shirt, which the stylist had bullied her into wearing so she'd look sexy. It hadn't worked. Tara could look cute on a good day, but she never looked sexy. T is behind her. He always had to be at the back in photos because he didn't look right. I can just make out an eye and a nostril poking out from his dreadlocks. When I spoke to Jane the other day, she said that she'd heard a rumor that T had shaved his dreads off, but I couldn't believe it. T without matted strands of hair was like Ant without Dec—wrong on so many levels.

And lastly, there's Dean on my left, looking every inch the rock star. He's wearing a secondhand Hawaiian shirt, and his hands are in the pockets of his trousers, and he's hunched his shoulders slightly to work the tortured-artist thing. His dark brown hair is the usual mop-top riot. He'd been experimenting with a mixture of Brylcreem and coconut wax that month to get his hair to the desired level of messiness. Even now, when I smell coconut, I think of Dean and remember him glooping it through his hair and getting Jane to pull and tug at his curls while she bitched about getting her fingers greasy. I'm beginning to wish I hadn't looked at the photo. It's making my stomach clench and knot. I rub a hand across my belly, trying to massage the taut flesh.

There's a polite cough behind me. Charles, my lawyer, has come back from the stationery cupboard where he was finding me a notebook. He places it on the table with a selection of pens. Not crappy Biros either but really nice fiber tips. No wonder he's so expensive. He pats me gingerly on the shoulder.

"Nothing to worry about, Molly," he assures me. "Just write everything down."

"Everything?" I sigh. "I don't know if I can remember much."

Charles gestures to the folders on the table. "They should jog your memory," he points out. "But you need to be thorough. Even incidents and conversation that don't seem important may help your case."

I pull a face but nod unwillingly. I know I'm being difficult, but I've spent the last few months on a blissful wave of denial, and now I have to relive the angst and betrayal all over again. No fair.

"OK, I'll get busy with pen and paper," I tell Charles, trying to keep my voice light and carefree.

"Good girl," he says. "And don't skip bits. I'll be in my office if you need me."

Another avuncular pat in the region of my shoulder, and he's gone. I turn over the cover of the notebook, and the snowy white page stares back at me. I pick up a pen, and I begin to write:

My name is Molly Montgomery. I'm nineteen years old, and I'm being sued for £5,000,000 by my former record company. . . .

I always thought that fame happened to other people. When I was little, all I wanted was to own a cake shop and spend my life surrounded by sticky buns. I'd eat chocolate eclairs for breakfast, lunch, and tea. But instead, I formed a band and became a rock 'n' roll star.

I suppose if I've learned something (besides never signing *anything* without a lawyer present and that sulky-faced boys will break your heart), it's that life takes funny turns when you're not looking. That Thursday afternoon was like every other Thursday afternoon. It was raining, and Jane and Tara and me had a free double period, I think, or maybe we were skiving off French because Jane hadn't done her homework. Anyway, we were hanging out in the music room because it was heated and had a great view of the back of the art college opposite, so we could gaze longingly at boys with strangely dyed hair who were sneaking a crafty cig. Jane was copying my French homework when she found this stupid poem I'd written about one of those boys with strangely dyed hair. So then she kept singing, "I want to be your highlighting cap" (I didn't say it was a good poem) over and over again in a high-pitched voice, and it was so annoying but catchy that the three of us spent the rest of the week humming the tune. That's how it started.

I know it was me who decided that we should form a band. I think I even said, "Hey, we should form a band." But we were always coming up with these ridiculous schemes to get a bit of respect. Not even respect, just to be *noticed* by someone. By anyone. Jane, at least, had a reputation—but that was only because she'd snogged even more boys than Lizzie Firestone. And Lizzie Firestone got away with it because she was blond and popular. Jane was also blond—but that was due to a monthly application of peroxide, and she wasn't popular, so it was all right for people to scrawl *Jane is a ho* on her locker. Me and Tara were completely anonymous; always picked last for games. The only thing that I was known for was being the only girl in the upper school who didn't need to wear a bra. So after staging a sit-down protest against having to dissect animals in biology (which no one attended) and performing an experimental art piece at the school's annual talent show (which resulted in detention and letters home), being in a band seemed like a logical progression.

I already had a guitar. It was a Christmas present that I'd begged and sulked for—and promptly discarded when I realized that strumming was going to wreck my nails. I dragged it out from under my bed, cut my nails right down, listened to my favorite songs over and over again, and worked out where to put my fingers on the fret board until I could play three chords.

Three chords was all that you really need, anyway. Ruby X— my heroine, my icon, everyone that I've ever wanted to be—once wrote this piece for one of the music papers about how there should be this girl revolution with girls starting bands in their bedrooms and taking over the world. They'd printed her scribbled diagram of lines and dots to illustrate three chords, and she'd scrawled the words underneath: *Now you can play the guitar.* It was our call to arms. Jane borrowed her brother's bass guitar and mastered one bass line, which we reckoned would do, and then we persuaded Tara to blow her baby-sitting money on a simple, stand-up drum kit. And the evenings that we usually spent watching *Buffy* reruns and whining about how everyone at school ignored us, were now spent writing songs and rehearsing.

The only problem was that we didn't know what to write songs about. Most songs are about love, and with the exception of Jane—who was the queen of the three-day relationship—me and Tara had barely even spoken to a boy. Ruby X always said that you should write about what you know. That worked for her because she'd been a stripper and hitchhiked across America when she was sixteen and had adventures. But I was just boring Molly Montgomery, flat-chested and never been kissed. Anyway, I wrote about what I knew. And what I knew was that boys never fancied you back, and that working weekends in the Best Buys convenience store was slowly sucking the soul out of me, and that there wasn't a problem in the world that couldn't be helped with copious amounts of chocolate. Put it this way, our songs didn't sound like anything I'd ever heard before.

Five weeks after that free period in the music room, we were a proper band. And we pretended it was because we were going to be part of the new girl revolution, but the truth was that being in a band was something we did in a desperate attempt to actually seem interesting. And we bullied Marie O'Sullivan into letting us play her sweet sixteen party 'cause it was the only way she could be sure that at least three people would definitely turn up.

Months later, everyone pretended that they'd been there—at our first ever gig. People at school who would usually pass us by in the corridors like we were made of air, and boys that we'd loved passionately but hadn't ever known we existed, even people who really should have known better—like journalists—all claimed to have attended. They were liars. Because that very first gig in Marie O'Sullivan's lounge never even made it into our record company biography—I mean, hello! Can you say uncool! It still managed to make it into the rock history books, though. There were ten people there (including two boys that Jane had met at the garage on the way and invited because everyone knew that Marie O'Sullivan's party was going to be geek central, and she wanted to guarantee a bit of boy action). We sang "Happy Birthday" and had time for one other song, "Hello Kitty Speedboat" (sample lyric: "Hello Kitty speedboat/You know how to float") before Mrs. O'Sullivan hustled us into the dining room for Jell-O and ice cream. God, that party *really* was geek central!

Jane had made us these freakish outfits out of this cheap silver material that had little red stars printed on it. You know that bit in *The Sound of Music* where the Von Trapp children roam around the streets of Salzburg wearing naff clothes that used to be curtains? We looked even more stupid than them. My dress was scratchy and stiff, and when I sat down, it made this squeaking noise against the vinyl chair, which sounded like I'd farted.

As we sat there, nursing bowls of supermarket own-brand strawberry ice cream and Jell-O that hadn't set properly, one of the boys from the garage paused from exchanging lingering eye contact with Jane to say to me, "So, like, what's your band called?"

The three of us looked at one another. I blushed right to the roots of my boring brown hair. Partly because a boy was actually talking to me, but mostly because we'd been so busy pretending that we were a proper band that we'd completely forgotten to think of a name.

"Um, well, we don't . . ." I started to mumble, but Jane fixed me with one of her "I'm in there, don't do anything to ruin it for me" glares and said smoothly, "We're called The Hormones because Molly here is a slave to hers."

I narrowed my eyes but decided to play along. "Yeah, pesky hormones," I muttered, and the garage boy seemed satisfied.

"Cool," he commented. "You were cool. So, do you want to come into the garden with me?" he added to Jane, and the two of them disappeared.

Two weeks later, I bumped into one of the boys from the garage as I stacked shelves in Best Buys. Instead of pretending he didn't know me, he was all smiles and conversation. His brother put on gigs at the local community center and did we want to play?

People in groups always pretend that they've had to suffer for their art, but we never did. Not at first, anyway. And right then, as I clutched cans of baked beans and beamed at the garage boy, anything seemed possible. Even getting through a whole thirty minutes on stage at the local community center.

The day before our first official gig, Jane nagged me to put a red rinse in my hair and wear something more exciting than jeans, but I ignored her. I was too busy trying to write a rousing, shouty song to finish our set with. It was about being a mermaid. In the end, Jane turned up on my doorstep with a packet of bleach and some Manic Panic hair dye in Very Cherry and dragged me into the bathroom, where she shoved a chair under the door handle. I reluctantly let her massacre my brown hair while my little brother, Joss, banged on the door.

"What are you doing in there, Moll?" he whined. "I really need to wee, and if you don't let me in, I'm telling on you."

When we very reluctantly opened the door and he caught sight of my fire-engine red hair, he yelped excitedly and then went and grassed me up to my parents. They were so glad that I was finally showing a bit of normal teen rebellion that Dad went and got his stupid digital camera and decided to record the moment for posterity. And when Jane informed them that we were in a band (I only ever tell my parents the finer details of my life on a strictly need-to-know basis), they got all misty-eyed and started reminiscing about their honeymoon at the Isle of Wight festival. I'll probably moan about my parents in greater detail later, but right then their crunchy granola-sponsored trip down memory lane made me irritable and sulky for the rest of the day.

I only started to freak out in the dressing room just before we went on stage. I'd decided to wear my Best Buys Bri-nylon overall as this cool ironic statement, but it was sticking to my fishnet tights in a very unflattering way, and I couldn't help but wonder if people would simply think I hadn't had time to change after work.

"I look like a dork, don't I?" I muttered for the fifty-seventh time, but Jane was back combing her hair and Tara was mumbling something about picturing the audience naked. I could taste the fear at the back of my throat. It was a metallic, bitter tang that wouldn't budge, no matter how much water I gulped down. I felt like I was about to go naked into battle.

But once I was actually on stage, it was too late to feel frightened. In actual fact, the warm glow of the spotlights felt comforting and safe, and it wasn't as if I could actually see anybody's faces. It was like being back in my bedroom but with much, much better lighting. Plus there was applause and shouts of encouragement, and for about the first time in my life, I felt like I belonged somewhere.

Then my feet, which had been rooted to the floor, began to move—and the next thing I knew, I was throwing definite rock chick shapes. One leg up on the monitor, head flung back, and my hips were shaking in a definite 'come hither' way, while I poured out all those words that had been stuck inside me for so long. . . .

"This is a song about those little toys that you get in the plastic egg machine outside Sainsbury's," I suddenly announced, like I'd been working a room since I was knee-high to a mic stand. "It's called 'Made in Korea.' One, two . . . One, two, three, four!" Jane was looking at me in disbelief and then shaking her head and laughing. And all the while I could feel the power thrumming through me, because I could make these noises come out of my guitar and make people listen to the stories inside my head.

After we came off stage, I didn't know where to put myself. All the adrenaline that had kicked in was still whooshing around my system. I prowled around the tiny dressing room 'cause it was such a kick to have a dressing room to prowl around in—but then Jane burst in, her usual cool abandoned. "There are people out there who want to talk to us!" she announced. "Stuck-up people who'd usually look down their noses at us. Are you coming, Moll?" But I was already out the door and trying to adjust my excited skipping to a more casual saunter.

"You were great."

"Loved the set."

"Are you playing again?"

"You're in my A-level psychology class."

I was surrounded by a blur of faces all talking at me, and I realized that this is what it must be like if you're popular. This is what it must be like if you're Lizzie Firestone or Tania Chase or all those other girls at school who fit in.

Jane came up behind me and wrapped a hot, sticky arm around my waist, and we talked to people who were actually interested in us and listened to us, pretending that we did this kind of thing every day. The last admirer (note to self: we had admirers!) eventually trailed away and I nudged Jane with my hip. "Being in a band is like a cheap day return to cool," I shouted in her ear.

She grinned. "And did you notice how they were all girls and they all looked a bit like us?"

"'Cept they weren't us, 'cause we—"

"'Cause we rock!"

We paused to ponder just how much we did rock when Tara suddenly appeared, looking all whey-faced and wan.

"I'm never doing that again," she said with a shudder. "Everyone was staring at us. Urgh!"

"What did you think they were going to do—close their eyes while we played?" Jane raised her eyes to heaven.

"I hadn't thought about it."

"Aw, poor Tara," I said, giving her hand a squeeze. "What happened to imagining them naked?"

Tara shuddered again. "I was too busy trying not to throw up to think about that."

Jane snorted and started to tell Tara how we were the new queens of the scene, but I was distracted by a boy. A boy who was staring at me like I was an all-you-can-eat buffet. I mean, he wasn't even making a paltry attempt to disguise the fact that he was staring at me—but I supposed I was going to have to get used to this kind of attention.

What would Ruby X do in this situation?

I sidled over to him, and as I got nearer I realized that apart from the unnerving starey thing, he was quite cute. Tall and lanky, but somehow managing to bypass weedy. Dark tufty hair, good cheekbones, and a T-shirt that would have looked like Hello Kitty if Hello Kitty had devil horns and a blood mustache.

He didn't stop looking as I closed the gap between us, just raised his eyebrows and waited for me to say something.

"Are you going to stare at me all night or are you going to buy me a drink?" My opening line was a nice blend of confrontation and flirtiness, I thought. I smiled mysteriously at him and wondered where I'd got the stones to be so . . . *sultry*.

"I'm going to stare," he said flatly, looking down his slightly-too-big nose at me.

"Oh." But the thing was, I couldn't walk away now that he'd fronted me, so I tried again. "Did you like our set?"

Starey-boy considered the question for a moment. "Your songs are really immature, you can't play your guitar to save your life, your drummer's a shambles, and as for the girl on bass—my gran could do better, and she's paralyzed down her right side."

I stood there, opening and shutting my mouth like a mentally challenged goldfish, racking my brains for a snappy, devastatingly brutal comeback to wipe the smirk off his face. But Jane, who must have been listening to his snark for some time, beat me to it.

"Well, screw you then, sad boy," she snarled. "I saw you gawping at Molly all through the set, and if you think slagging us off is gonna get her interested, then you're even more lame than you look."

"Yeah," I added, all brave and blustery now that my best friend had appeared.

The boy looked unimpressed. "You're going to have to get

used to constructive criticism if you're serious about your, um, group," he said, smirking again.

How could I ever have thought that he was cute? "We *are* serious," I said witheringly.

"I bet you thought you'd get loads of little groupies, didn't you?" he continued. "And that you'd be the heroines of the Year Twelve common room tomorrow."

Jane had given up any attempt to speak, but from the way she kept clenching and unclenching her fists I could tell she was planning to inflict bodily harm.

"Look, you don't know anything about us—" I began angrily, but sounds were still coming out of his mouth.

"I know you need a decent guitarist and a drummer who's not afraid to beat the crap out of his kit." He turned to Tara, who'd wandered over to see what was going on. "No offense."

"None taken. I suck," she agreed happily. Jane and I glared at her furiously.

"Tara," growled Jane warningly.

"I'm Dean, by the way," said the boy, as if we actually cared.

"And we're *so* not interested," Jane hissed.

All my adrenaline had fizzled away after Hello Satan's little pep talk was done. I turned to walk away, but Dean grabbed my arm. I looked at his hand like it was made of some icky, radioactive gloop.

"You need me," he said simply.

I rolled my eyes. "Look, I can get better at playing the guitar, but you really have to work on your social skills," I snapped back. Hell, yeah, I could still cut a boy down to size! Eventually.

Dean's mouth twisted at the corners in a faint approximation of a smile. "Who says I was talking about your guitar playing?" he murmured in a low voice so only I could hear. And while I was trying to figure out what the hell he meant by *that*, he came out with something so audacious that Jane and I could only stand there and blink.

"Me and my mate T will come to your next rehearsal. We'll show you how good you can sound," Dean said, as if it was a foregone conclusion rather than a suggestion.

I looked at Jane expectantly for the "Drop dead, creep" retort that she was probably working on, but she pulled a face and shrugged. I turned back to Dean, who raised an eyebrow—and I just knew that he'd practiced that move in his mirror.

"Give me your number and maybe I'll call you," I sighed reluctantly. I'd already known this guy for all of two minutes and I hated the sight of him. Him joining the band and spending quality time with us didn't really seem like a viable option, but he was already scrabbling in the pockets of his jean jacket for something to write on.

"Or maybe I'll just pay someone to kick your arse," I continued under my breath. He suddenly looked up and gave me this blinding smile that illuminated his whole face, and I knew that he'd heard me.

In the end it was Tara who called Dean, so it was all her fault really. She hated playing the drums and wanted to trade in her kit for this cute little seventies keyboard she'd found in a charity shop.

"Him and his mate are coming round tomorrow," she said casually as we were walking to French and pretending that we weren't aware of the cluster of Year Nine girls who'd been following us and laughing at my pink Converse All Stars—which were pretty out there for downtown Southport, I admit.

"To *my* house?" I squeaked. "I don't like the thought of that boy in my room, sneering at my posters and sitting on my bed."

"He's coming round to do music stuff," Tara commented mildly. "Not diss your choice of soft furnishings."

"I don't like him," I grumbled. "He's arrogant and bossy and his friend is probably just the same. And they'll just take over the band—and we're meant to be part of the girl revolution."

"But he's kinda cute," Tara said. "And other bands can probably play more than three chords. Even bands who are part of the girl revolution."

"But he's so, so, so . . . I can't quite think of the word, Tar. Aggressive, confrontational, jerky—all fine words but not really capturing his essential arseholeness. His friend's probably even worse."

But Tara just smiled in this maddening way, like she'd just remembered the punch line to a really funny joke but didn't think that I'd get it. And then it was all verb conjugations and trying to write a critique of *le train* versus *l'autobus*. It wasn't until later that night, when I was trying to explain to my parents why they should break their house rule and let me have boys in my room, that I remembered that this Dean thing was not a good idea.

My parents like to think they're holdover hippies because they went to a couple of festivals when they were at university. They claim to be liberal and want me and Joss to "follow your own paths in life" —but that's just a great stinking lie. 'Cause after five years of non-gender-specific toys, Joss spends all his time trying to make weapons of mass destruction out of (biodegradable) washing-up liquid bottles and recyclable toilet rolls. It makes Mum cry and wonder if she should take him to a child psychologist. And I'm a disappointment because I spend all my time moping about in my bedroom, being apathetic. Plus I work in Best Buys instead of toiling away in the non-profit-making organic food shop they own—their shop being why we have no money and live on a starvation diet of mung beans and chickpeas. No wonder I'm stunted.

But like every other parent on the planet, they can be relentlessly unyielding about their precious house rules. Mostly it's trivial stuff like not hoarding mugs in my room until they grow enough mold to support their own ecosystem. But I did get grounded for a month once when Dad saw me coming out of McDonald's (or that "evil capitalist empire that makes billions out of the slaughter of innocent animals," as it's catchily known in our house) clutching a Happy Meal. And the boy rule is set in stone. Which is stupid, really, because the last boy who willingly came into my room was Tim Binks when I was seven, and that was to play Barbies (a present from my very gender-specific grandma) together. Tim's now a member of the Army Cadet Force and runs as fast as his stumpy legs will carry him whenever he sees me.

"It's two boys, and Jane and Tara will be there too," I tried to explain. "It's a band thing."

"Molly, we don't have rules for the sake of it," said my mother in her reasonable voice. "Rules are about respecting other people."

I rolled my eyes. "I am respecting you," I muttered between gritted teeth. "You're not respecting me. Or listening to me. I'd keep the door open the whole time they're here, but then you'd complain about the noise."

"I don't know why you need to use an amp in your bedroom," my dad added. "Bob Dylan didn't need any amplification."

It was at moments like this that I knew I had to be adopted. There was no biological way I could share DNA with these two people. I actually had a theory that I'd sprung forth fully formed from the froth of the ocean, but my birth certificate tended to discount that theory.

"Because I like it better when I can't actually hear myself

sing," I whimpered. "Look, could you please, please, please be flexible about this? You're both acting like a pair of power-crazed fascists."

And that was about the worst thing I could call my parents because (as they never tire of telling me) they marched on Whitehall to ban the bomb and stop apartheid and generally make the world a better place for me. Name-calling is not big or clever, but at least it made my parents give in and realize the world would only be a better place for me if they let me have boys in my bedroom.

So the next day after school, I tried to ignore the feeling in my stomach as Jane and Tara set up the drum kit and we waited for Dean and T to arrive. It wasn't a good feeling. It was more like an I'm-going-to-be-violently-sick feeling, which got worse and worse as I looked around my bedroom and tried not to think about how immature and crap it would look to boys who wear satanic Hello Kitty T-shirts.

I still have the flower-sprigged wallpaper up that I've had since primary school, and though it was now practically obscured by posters of Ruby X, the whole room looked like I'd tried for a good-girl-gone-bad style and failed miserably. Then I looked at Jane, who always looks cool with her bleached hair and pierced lip and teeny tops and baggy trousers. And then I looked at Tara, who lags behind even me in her ineffectual attempts to look like anything other than a gawky sixteen-year-old. And then I looked down at my scruffy old jeans and the blue school shirt I'd filched from Joss's room, which should not have done up except for my utter lack of breastage. One hand crept up to my ponytail in horror. Oh, God, we were a complete joke. Dean and his no doubt equally rude friend wouldn't be convinced by our talk about the girl revolution and three chords. They were going to suss out our amateur status the minute they walked through the door.

But it was worse than that. Because the doorbell went and before I could scurry down at twice the speed of light, my dad was there first. And I could hear him wittering on as three pairs of feet climbed the stairs. ". . . There's only one guy who ever shook the world with his music, and that man was Bob Dylan! I mean, have you heard *Blood on the Tracks?*"

I closed my eyes for a second and then scrambled for the door in time to hear Dean say, "I actually prefer *Nashville Skyline*." Trust him to be able to slime up to my dad by bonding over whiny-voiced singers from the sixties.

"It's OK, Dad, I can take it from here," I hissed as he reached the landing. "Downstairs NOW!"

"No need to be like that, Mopsy," said the stupid man who claimed paternity of me.

I just knew Dean was smirking. I couldn't see his face, only the torn shoulder of his green sweater as he hovered somewhere behind my father, but I could tell he was smirking.

"I've told you a million times not to call me that," I managed to bite out, as I reached around and grabbed Dean by the arm and made a "through there" gesture with my head toward the open door. "Daaaad!"

With a slightly hurt shrug of his shoulders, which I wasn't buying for a second, my dad was turning toward the stairs. I followed the mysterious T into my room.

T was as quiet and hairy as Dean was talkative and sneery. He grunted at Jane and Tara, who were sitting on my bed, and shook his head forward so that his face was even more obscured by his dirty blond dreads.

"This is T," Dean said, slouching against my dressing table and looking at the precise point down the side of my bed where I'd shoved all my soft toys. "So that was your dad?"

"No," I squealed. "That man is a science project that went horribly, horribly wrong, and I don't want to talk about it."

"Whatever," Dean replied.

In the end it wasn't that bad. I mean the awkward introductions were bad, and my mum popping up to see "if your little friends would like some organic apple juice" was excruciating, but it got better.

Dean had brought his acoustic guitar and suggested that we play a couple of our songs and that he'd figure out the chords (like *that* was going to be rocket science) and join in, and T would do percussion. And the weird thing was that it worked. "Hello Kitty Speedboat" sounded all poignant and sad when Dean played it, and he changed some of the notes around. T altered the beat in "Toxic," and it started to sound catchy and actually have a chorus. We sounded like a proper group, which shocked me so much that I promptly forgot the words.

I didn't want Dean to know that, though. He was a genius at the guitar, I'd give him that, but the hour that he stayed confirmed my first impressions: He was a major pain in the butt. And bossy with it. I thought Jane was bossy. Actually I know for a fact that Jane is bossy, but the arrogant way that Dean ordered us around, changed lyrics that he didn't like, and rummaged through my CD collection without asking was way worse than Jane nagging me to go and tell boys that she fancied them.

There was no way he was joining the band. T could join the band, if he was just going to sit there and be a good drummer, but Dean just wouldn't work out—not without me beating him to death with my mini amp at some point.

"So, we'll call you, OK?" I said as Dean packed up his guitar. He glanced at me and I realized that his eyes were the exact same shade of gray as my old school uniform.

"Well, why wait?" he wanted to know. "You sounded tons better, you know you did."

"We did," I admitted. "But we're a girl band. We're about being girls. Aren't we?"

Jane raised her eyebrows. "Yup, all about being girls. It's like our *raison d'être* or something."

"How?" Dean said, folding his arms.

"How what?" I asked dumbly, looking down at the frayed bottoms of his jeans.

"How are you about being girls? I mean, how is writing songs about toys and Hello Kitty about being a girl?"

I nibbled the edge of my nail. "Well, it just is. Because . . . because . . . because we're not writing songs about boy stuff and love, or we are, but it's different because we're using Hello Kitty as this metaphor. Anyway, we're part of the girl revolution and only knowing three chords, and it's none of your business, anyway!" I finished this irrational statement on an angry intake of breath.

Dean narrowed his eyes and looked at me again, like he was trying to guesstimate my net value on *Antiques Roadshow.* "Well, if you feel like that . . ."

"We do," I said firmly. "It was good to jam with you but—"

"Hold on," interrupted Jane. "This is a democracy not a Mollyocracy. Don't Tara and I get a say?"

I frowned. What was Jane getting so pissed off about? She thought the same as me. She had to. Unless she fancied Dean or T. There was no other reason why she'd want to be in a band with them.

"Well, maybe T doesn't want to be in the band either," I stalled, trying to play for time until I got Jane on her own and could ask her what the hell she was playing at.

T shrugged, then nodded, and finally tossed his dreads gently back and forth. I looked at Dean for clarification.

"He's in," Dean told me with a certain amount of satisfaction. "Jane's in. I'm in. While you were in the loo, Tara was telling me that she couldn't wait to give up the drums and try out her new keyboard, so it looks like you're the one who's out."

"Jeez, Molly, we sounded miles better," whined Jane impatiently. "You know we did. And, I'd rather be in a band with boys in it that rocks than be in a girl band that sucks."

It had only been ninety minutes since Dean walked through the door, and he'd already managed to turn Jane and Tara against me and kick me out of my own band. Oh, God, how I hated him! I could feel my lower lip jutting out in the mother of all pouts.

"It's simple, Moll," said Dean, touching me lightly on the shoulder in a way that made me shudder with revulsion. "Are you in or are you out?"

There was a moment of silence, while everyone waited for my reply. I was kind of enjoying the dramatic tension and, for a moment, thought about having a huge hissy fit and telling them to stuff the band as I was going to embark on a successful solo career. But that would have been way too melodramatic. Besides, I liked being in a band. I liked walking down the street with Jane and Tara as if we were a cool gang with a mission, instead of three girls with half an hour to kill before the end of lunch break. And we did sound better with Dean and T, though they were older than us and had probably had more time to work on their music. Hmmm, it was a pity they hadn't applied the same dedication to their people skills while they were at it.

"Earth to Molly. Earth to Molly." My reverie was interrupted by Jane. "So, in or out?"

I sighed long and deep. "In, I guess."

If this was a movie (and Charles has suggested selling the film rights to my story so I get to make a little bit of money out of the whole fiasco), there'd now be this cute montage of the months that followed. Our song "Magic Marker Love" would be playing in the background, and there'd be shots of me sitting in my art history class and biting my pencil to show that I was absorbing all that painty knowledge. Then there'd be a shot of Dean and T flipping burgers in their McJob. Cut to Jane re-dyeing my hair red over our bathroom sink while Tara sits on the toilet bowl trying to turn off the bossa nova beat button on her keyboard. Cut to Dean and me sitting in the park with our guitars, surrounded by scraps of paper. Cut to Dean stalking off and leaving me to ball up the scraps of paper and chuck them at his retreating back. Cut to T asleep in the corner of the rehearsal room we are hiring, and Tara holding her pocket mirror over his mouth to check that he is still breathing. And, finally, cut to all five of us in the rehearsal room actually playing "Magic Marker Love," which takes us right up to the point where my fingers run like liquid over the fret board to shape that difficult fourth chord I never knew I could play.

> *It could have been that there wasn't much on telly*
> *When I magic-markered your name across my belly*
> *I drew a heart over the I*
> *And I knew I'd love you till the day I died.*

And then we all stopped playing at the same time, just like proper bands do.

I pulled my guitar strap over my head and gently placed my guitar on its stand, before stretching tiredly. We'd been playing that song for two hours straight.

"We are so ready to play live," Jane announced. "Don't you think, Dean?"

Dean made all the decisions in the band now because he was a power-crazed despot. He said it was easier that way, especially after he'd gently pointed out that it took Tara and me at least an hour to decide what we wanted to eat during our midrehearsal snack breaks. He ran his fingers through his already tousled hair and dropped to the floor with a groan, his arms outstretched so his T-shirt rode up and we could all see his stomach and the top of his boxer shorts. I looked away quickly, as the gap between his T-shirt and his jeans made me feel *squicky.* Maybe it was because the carpet in the rehearsal room was covered in black gunge and squelched slightly if you jumped up and down on it.

"Yeah, I think we're ready," Dean agreed.

He'd been the one who decided that we shouldn't play any more gigs till we could actually play and, you know, in between studying for A levels and working in Best Buys and rehearsing, it was easier to go along with what Dean wanted.

"But we shouldn't play third on the bill of some crappy local bands night," Dean continued. "We have to launch ourselves carefully. Get a real buzz going. Make *them* come to us."

I didn't need to ask who "them" was. We weren't three girls playing at being guitar-wielding revolutionaries anymore. Dean and T were deadly serious about being in the band and becoming famous. And "them" were scary music business types who were going to come down from London to our small town, discover us, and deliver us from a life of flipping burgers and conjugating French verbs. That was the plan. Dean had spelled it out to me one night after rehearsal when I'd wanted to go home early because I had an English test the next day. He decided that I had commitment issues about being in the band. Needless to say I'd got a C on my test.

"So what's a suitable way to launch ourselves?" I asked. "The Richmond's having a Battle of the Bands contest in a couple of weeks. We could go in for that."

Dean slumped flat on the floor and groaned. "You have to think bigger than that, Molly. Battle of the Band competitions are for losers. Everybody gets their mates down to cheer and some soft rock covers band always wins."

"And we don't have any friends," added Jane helpfully. "Well, not enough to fix the voting, anyway."

I caught Tara's eye and we pulled faces at each other. Jane always agreed with everything Dean said.

"It was an idea that's all," I muttered dully. "Silly me."

Dean suddenly sprang to his feet, as if the exhausted sprawling on the floor had been just an act, and blocked my path toward the door.

"Hey, c'mon, don't be like that," he cajoled, reaching out to touch my arm where the sleeve of my Best Buys uniform ended. "We're all tired, but that was a great rehearsal and you were fantastic, Moll." And then Dean smiled at me. And the last couple of months have taught me that although Dean can be more irritating than a sudden outbreak of nits, he can also make you feel like the most important person in the world. When he smiles at you and his eyes crinkle up and you can see the chipped front tooth (legacy of a nasty accident with the edge of the grill and a bucket of industrial chip fat at work apparently), it's like being bathed in sunlight. You end up getting all starry-eyed in the face of Dean's approval, even when you really, really don't want to. He'd make a great motivational speaker. And he's goal orientated. In fact, if he hadn't set his heart on rock 'n' roll glory, a career in politics would have been a natural choice.

I could feel my sulkiness melt away until I was dipping my head and going pink at the edges and generally being a total girl.

"Sorry, people," I said. "I'm a total bitch queen from Bitchonia."

"Yeah, but you're our bitch queen, so that's all right," said Jane, coming up behind me and tugging at the end of my ponytail. "And Dean's got this fantastic idea for our first gig as the new and improved Hormones. He was telling me earlier . . . go on, Dean."

Dean pushed me gently down into a sitting position on an amp, so he could have optimum pacing space.

Dean's fantastic plan was to support Bikini Dust. Bikini Dust were our biggest local band, who'd almost had a couple of Top Forty hits, and were still doing the Britpop thing seven years after it had gone out of fashion. I thought our "in" would be down to Jane, who'd snogged one of their roadies at a Christmas party, but apparently T had done some session work on their last album (for someone who doesn't talk much he sure gets around). He'd given their manager a tape Dean had made of one of our rehearsals. They wanted us to open for them at this secret homecoming gig they were planning to wind up their latest tour.

"It's invitation only," gloated Dean. "You don't get more exclusive than that. There's bound to be loads of industry people there."

"That sounds cool," commented Tara, looking as if she was about to throw up. "Lots of cool industry people being cool. Great."

I could tell Dean was waiting for my reaction and I had to hand it to him. He knew what he was doing. It made my Battle of the Bands seem completely lame with added bits of lameness.

"You're such an operator," I finally said with grudging admiration. "It beats Marie O'Sullivan's sweet sixteen party."

And then Dean frowned and told me for the millionth time that if anyone asked us where we played our first gig, Marie O'Sullivan's sweet sixteen party never happened.

It was weird how quickly things happened after that. Like we were going downhill in a car and the brakes had failed and all we could do was pick up speed and hope that our seat belts worked.

The Bikini Dust show was everything Dean had hoped it would be. We soared that night. All those tedious, painful rehearsals had been worth it.

As I stepped up to the mic in the white minidress that my mum had got married in (and which Jane would later spill lager on) and said, "We're The Hormones and we've come to steal your souls," there was an audible hum in the room. It got louder and louder as we blazed our way through the set, and then exploded into clapping and cheering and people going, "Woo woo!"

When Tara and I tried to get to the bar after we came off stage, we found we couldn't walk more than two paces without getting pounced on by record company types who wanted our people to call their people. When we did eventually make it to the bar, we found Dean deep in conversation with this ridiculously handsome, twenty-something guy in a sharp suit who was clutching Dean's wrist as if he was scared he was going to run off. As he caught sight of me, he let go of Dean and grabbed my arm so he could pull me toward him.

"Here she is," he exclaimed excitedly. "This is the biggest star in the room."

"Actually I'm mostly going by the name of Molly these days," I shouted over the noise of Bikini Dust murdering a Beatles song. And Dean smirked because part of his plan was that I should be all attitudey and bad girl.

"This is Paul," Dean said. "He wants to manage us."

And with those eight words everything changed. I didn't realize that something monumental had happened. You never recognize those big moments when they happen, it's only afterward when you look back and wonder at the weirdness that you realize. Right then, I sipped a Diet Coke, which someone had thrust into my hand, and nodded and smiled as Paul talked at me and Dean about how he was going to make us famous.

When you're seventeen, not many people bother to tell you that you're special. I mean, your parents do, but that's their job. Listening to Paul bang on and on about how wonderful I was and what a great voice I had and how unique my lyrics were and "that dress—it's inspired" was more addictive than crack cocaine. Probably. I've never actually done crack cocaine, but I saw a documentary about it once in health.

Finally, Jane and Tara dispatched T over to us, who conveyed with a series of head shakes and dreadlock rustling that the van was double-parked and we had to go.

Dean started to panic about finding paper and a pen, but Paul reached into his suit, pulled out one of those complicated pocket computers, and looked at me with one long finger poised over the keypad.

"Can I get your digits?" he asked, smiling at me and winking.

"Huh?" I frowned, thrown by the wink and "digits."

Dean nudged me viciously. "Your phone number," he hissed. "Give him your number."

I supplied the information and couldn't help but smirk as Dean gave Paul his mobile number, his home phone number, his McJob number, and his e-mail address. He would probably have insisted that Paul tapped in the number of the rehearsal room too, but I tugged on his sleeve.

"Dean, we have to go! Double-parked, remember?"

"We'll talk soon," Paul promised, and as I stuck out my hand in a vague way in case he wanted to shake it, he leaned down and kissed me on the cheek. He smelled of cigarettes and citrus. I was just thinking about how sophisticated the kiss and the smell was when Dean grabbed my arm and began to pull me away, muttering about how all these music business types were full of it.

But Paul wasn't full of it. When I got home from school the next day, he was sitting in our living room, making awkward conversation with my mother and not drinking the glass of elderflower cordial that she'd made. I'd forgotten how ridiculously, male-model kind of good-looking he was. He looked like he should have been striding across a deserted beach advertising aftershave in an open white shirt and faded jeans, with his blond hair ruffling attractively in the breeze. I could tell that Mum was wishing that she'd dragged a brush through her bird's nest mop and applied the one lipstick she owned.

"What are you doing here?" I yelped, chucking my schoolbag on the floor and noting that I didn't even get yelled at for doing it like most days. Instead, Mum jumped up and hugged me.

"Paul's just been telling me about your gig last night," she cried. "You should have told us. We'd have loved to have been there."

Paul smiled faintly into his glass. He knew that was precisely why I hadn't told them.

"It was no big deal," I muttered, shrugging and trying to dislodge her arms.

"It's a very big deal," Mum gushed. She turned to Paul and made an apologetic face. "She's at that difficult age where they're negative about everything, but Molly's a very special girl."

Paul nodded. "My thoughts exactly," he said with another little smile. My mother beamed. I scowled.

"Your father's on his way home," Mum informed me. "This is all so exciting. Your little band, Molly. You'll be just like that woman you like, Ruby S—"

"Ruby X," I growled.

"Molly plays her music all the time. I think I must know all the words to her songs by now. . . ."

I heard a key turn in the lock. Saved by the dad, I thought darkly as Paul stared at the framed anti-Vietnam poster on the wall in bemusement.

Dad took one look at Paul in his fancy suit and his face tightened at the sight of the capitalist running dog sitting on his sofa.

"Mr. Montgomery," Paul said, standing up and offering Dad his hand. Dad took it and shook it gingerly.

"What's going on here?" Dad asked belligerently, like we were about to co-opt him into a satanic ritual.

"Paul saw Molly's band last night," Mum began. "He wants her to go to London and me—" she didn't get very far when Dad held up his hand in a needlessly dramatic way.

"Sheila, can I have a word—in the kitchen?" he said, and dragged her off, shutting the door firmly behind him.

"You don't have to drink that," I told Paul, who was still standing in the middle of the room, clutching his glass. "It tastes disgusting."

Paul slopped the pink liquid around a bit and then placed the drink on our coffee table.

"Your mum seems very nice," he commented, sitting down again.

"She's OK," I conceded grudgingly. "How did you find me? I never gave you my address."

Paul tapped the side of his nose. "Ah, I have my sources. So how do you fancy playing a gig in London?"

I was just about to say that it would thrill me to my very core when the sound of Dad shouting made me lose my conversational thread.

"You don't know anything about the guy! He's just some flash git in an expensive suit trying to impress us small town hicks. Molly has school and university after that and if you think . . ."

Paul and I looked at each other uncomfortably. I strode over to the door and yanked it open. "You know we can hear every word you're saying!" I yelled.

There was a brief silence, and then they came back in, both of them looking a little shamefaced.

"I know this all sounds a bit out of the blue," Paul jumped in. "And I know Molly has commitments, but I'm just talking about one little gig. We'll pay her expenses, make sure she's looked after."

"And who's 'we'?" Dad asked in a grumpy voice.

"I work for a music management company," Paul said. "If we represented Molly and her band, we'd get them a record deal, look after their day-to-day affairs. I manage some other bands: Bikini Dust, Mellowstar, The Flaming Daisies."

Mum and Dad looked blank. "We're a bit out of touch," Mum explained.

Paul smiled calmy and got up from the sofa in one smooth movement. "I understand that this is a bit of a shock, but I believe Molly's very talented. She could have a big future. Why don't you take my card, check me out, and give me a ring in a couple of days?"

He reached into his jacket and pulled out a business card, which he handed to Dad, who took it like Paul was offering him a processed meat product. Then in a whirl of citrus aftershave and tailored Armani suitage, he was gone. And, boy, did I have some explaining to do.

* * * * * * PRESS RELEASE * * * * * *

THE Hormones

MONSTER RECORDS are proud to announce the release of the debut single from Southport band **The Hormones** on 14 February.

The *Hey, Hey, We're The Hormones* EP features 'Toxic,'

which has already been playlisted on Radio 1, and live favourites 'Magic Marker Love,' 'Hello Kitty Speedboat,' and 'Bob Dylan Ate My Father.'

Discovered supporting fellow Southporters Bikini Dust at a secret gig, The Hormones are Molly Montgomery (17) on vocals and guitar, Dean Speed (19) lead guitar, Jane Fabian (18) bass, Tara Jenkin (17) keyboards, and the mysterious T (20) on percussion. In fact, owing to the youth of the two youngest Hormones, their parents had to sign their recording contracts for them.

'My mum and dad were a bit pissed off when they got a note from the school saying that I was answering my mobile in lessons to talk to A & R men, but they're one hundred percent behind us,' said Molly, before adding that she no longer gets grounded because it cuts into rehearsal time!

Formed a year ago in Molly's bedroom, The Hormones have played only a handful of live dates but have created a buzz that saw them signing an exclusive management deal only days after their first London show.

The band will be showcasing the *Hey, Hey, We're The Hormones* EP with a one-off London gig before returning to Southport, where Molly and Tara will be sitting their A levels. Rock 'n' roll, phew!

There will be an album and a national tour later on in the year.

For interview requests and promos call:
Bee Bee on 0727580623

• • •

Paul phoned Dean the next day to say that he'd organized a gig for us in London so we could play to a bigger crowd and meet his boss. And although my A-level mocks were less than a month away, I hissy-fitted and sulked until the 'rental units agreed to let me go to London. And it all came true, just like it said in the record company press release. Well, sort of.

I *did* get pulled out of a French class by the school secretary, but it wasn't an A & R man on the phone, it was Dean pretending to be my brother and demanding to know why my dad hadn't returned Paul's phone calls. All that stuff about my parents being 100 per-cent behind us? Not even close! There was a tortuous two weeks of family councils before Dad would even meet with Paul again. And then he only agreed to *maybe consider* me intermitting for a year if the band took off because in between talking to Dean on the phone and whining, I wasn't getting any revision done. It was hard to sit him and Mum down and explain that the band wasn't just an after-school activity to look good on my UCAS form and that I needed to get a lawyer and an accountant and, oh yeah, a PR. And I'm a recording artist without a recording contract be-cause yeah, I'm too young to sign it and Dad has a problem with authority figures (ironic much) and won't meet with a solicitor.

So while I sat in a freezing cold exam room and tried to remem-ber what *To Kill a Mockingbird* teaches us about the corruption of in-nocence, Dean and T were handing in their notices at the McJob, Jane was telling our headmaster exactly what he could do with his A-level syllabus, and Paul was conference calling with a copy of our demo tape and no less than three major record companies.

It would have been really exciting if I hadn't had to worry about my stupid mocks. Real life was so, well, *real*—what with the exams and school (though the hordes of Year Nine kids whispering about me in the lunch queue was starting to seriously freak me out). I felt as if the wiggy other world of record company expense-account lunches in Southport's only four-star restaurant and Paul offering to buy me a £1,000 guitar was happening to someone else. I'd lie in bed trying to sleep and instead get up and look in the mirror to reassure myself that I was still me. The pale-faced girl who looked back at me with the Very Cherry hair and a worried expression didn't look like the subject of a record company bidding war.

Talk about the record deal had simmered down at school. After the five-minute wonder of us being in the band, everyone had gone back to ignoring us, and with Jane locked away in her bedroom feverishly customizing secondhand clothes for our stage wear, there was only Tara and me left to wander the corridors and gaze at the boys from the art college opposite.

The Wednesday after our CD came out it was pouring down with rain, and as I trudged to the bus stop, I couldn't help but muse on how completely sucky life as a pop star was turning out. I was sure that Ruby X had never had to go to school in a downpour as she waited for the midweeks to come out.

The bus came and as I made my way to the upper deck and tried not to batter OAPs with my art portfolio case, I became aware of an excited whispering.

"That's her!"

"It can't be. She's not even pretty and there is no way that's her natural hair color."

I glanced at the two small girls, who I vaguely recognized

from the lower school. But as our eyes met, they both looked away. I mentally shrugged and found an empty seat toward the back of the bus. I was just adding up the numbers on my bus ticket to see if they came to twenty-one, when I became aware of the two girls padding purposefully up the aisle toward me. The grimly determined expressions on both their faces told me this wasn't a social call.

"Oi!" shouted the pudgy one before they were even within ten feet of me. "We want a word with you!"

I looked up unwillingly. "Me?" I said innocently.

"You in that band with the stupid name?" asked the second one belligerently.

"Um, what band would that be?" I asked timidly, wondering if I was about to get mugged for my record company advance, which was currently sitting in the newly created Hormones bank account. It was about enough to buy a bag of chips once the management fees, legal fees, and recording costs were deducted.

"The Hormones," said pudgy girl, scornfully. "There's this article in the local paper about how you go to our school, 'cept we'd never heard of you." She gestured at her friend. "But her brother reckons you're in his English class."

"Oh." I looked around helplessly to see if anyone was going to stop me being attacked by a pair of prepubescent harpies, but the other passengers were not making eye contact.

"So, like, are you in this band or what? Are you Molly?" asked pudgy girl's little mate.

I nodded, and they both scowled at me. I idly wondered if I could have them in a fight. Pudgy girl possibly, but her friend looked like she could get vicious.

"So why are you still going to school then?"

"Because I'm in the middle of doing my A levels," I huffed. "And I promised my parents that I'd finish school if they signed my contracts, and we're only a little band and . . . and . . . and it's none of your business."

I glared at them. I really didn't need an interrogation from two eleven-year-olds when I had double French in half an hour. Then I worried that they were going to beat me up and steal my lunch money.

"Sorry," they chorused, and looked like they kind of meant it. "It's just we were wondering if you'd met Britney Spears."

I shook my head in disbelief. "No, I haven't met Britney." Because she just never seemed to come into Best Buys when I was working my shift.

Pudgy girl shifted restlessly. "Well, when you do meet her, could you get us her autograph?"

I could feel this hysterical giggle starting somewhere in the region of my esophagus. "Sure, I can do that," I agreed. "Next time I bump into her."

"So then they asked me for my autograph," I told Dean, who was sitting on my bedroom floor with the music papers spread out before him. "And then they said that they were going to bunk off school and hang out at the Arndale Centre and did I want to come?"

"Tempting offer," he said mildly as he sipped a cup of chamomile tea supplied by my mother. "Y'know, I think I'm actually starting to like the taste of this stuff."

"It was so weird," I continued. "I thought they were going to demand my lunch money and bash me over the head with their hockey sticks. But they were really sweet."

"Hmmm, yeah . . . So do you want to read the reviews or do you want to go on some more about our preteen fan base?"

"I was just *saying,* Dean," I snapped. "So, OK, review me."

"I really think you should read them yourself," Dean said in such a strained voice that I looked up from painting my toenails sparkly purple. He was trying to assume his usual air of rock-star-in-waiting nonchalance but his legs were jiggling uncontrollably, and there was this funny tic thing happening just below his left eye.

"Are they that bad?" I gulped.

"Just read them," he repeated in that scary voice. I took my time screwing the top back on to the bottle of polish while Dean twitched and finally held out a hand for the papers, which he practically shoved into my grasp.

Reprinted by kind permission of *Music Maker* magazine

▮SINGLE OF THE WEEK▮▬▬

The Hormones
Hey, Hey, We're The Hormones EP
(Big Black Records)

Hey, hey, they're The Hormones and they've got something to say. And mostly it's about wiggy stuff like magic markers and Hello Kitty. This young band (Molly, the lead singer, isn't old enough to vote or get wasted on Jack Daniel's) are all whirling guitars,

> beeping noises, and choruses that end in
> 'yeah, yeah, yeah'—and might possibly be the
> future of rock 'n' roll. Even if they're not, ex-
> pect them to steal your hearts before the end
> of the month.

"God, why does everyone keep going on about how young I am?" I yelped indignantly. "Like, getting drunk is so mature."

Dean rolled his eyes. "Whatever," he drawled. "What about the review? We got *Single of the Week*! And *NME* have made us their Hot Tip! Crappy one in *The Hot List*, though."

"What does it say?"

"That your lyrics are like nursery rhymes," Dean told me carefully.

I shrugged. Nursery rhymes were OK—better than writing whiny mope-rock anthems like most of the bands that *The Hot List* championed.

"Doesn't it bother you?" Dean wanted to know.

I shook my head. "Nah, I've decided that to get caught up in all this would just be wrong. If I believed all the stuff that people are saying when we go for meetings, my head would get so big it'd probably explode." And I'd read this interview with Ruby X where she said that she used bad reviews to line her cat's litter tray—but I wasn't going to tell Dean that.

Dean raised his eyebrows. "That's very mature of you."

"Yeah, well . . ."

"'Cause our lyrics—they're *not* very mature, are they?" he continued.

"They're fun," I protested, leaning back on my arms so I could glare at Dean, who still looked all wrong in the flower-sprigged confines of my room. "Why should they have to make some big statement about world peace or get all tortured about love?"

"Paul thinks we should think about maturing our songs slightly, that's all," he said, just a bit too casually.

"He didn't say anything to me," I snapped, upgrading the glare to a full-on scowl.

"Since when do you speak to Paul? You usually just stare at him and flutter your eyelashes," Dean said nastily. This wasn't true and was very hurtful.

"If you must know, he calls me on my mobile at school every day." The record company had bought me a mobile so I could be available in an emergency and because I was the only teenager in Britain whose parents thought they were an invention of the devil. "Looking after my investment" was how Paul phrased it the first time he called. I looked forward to our chats as I waited for the bus and moaned about my parents' fascistic attitude toward homework.

"Oh," Dean said in a slightly less aggressive voice. "Well, he likes our songs but thinks some of your imagery is a bit too banal. Like, writing songs about cartoons and boys you have crushes on. It's a bit . . . *childish*, isn't it?"

"No! It's what I know. I'm sorry I don't have a more exciting life, but that's what makes us different. I'm not changing how I write, and I don't believe that Paul said that, and you're just making it up because you want to write the lyrics and take that over just like you've taken over everything else, and it's my band too, and you're just in it because you forced . . ." As I ranted on and on, Dean slid off the bed and stalked toward me.

"Shut up. Just shut up," he demanded in a tight voice.

"God, you're so bossy. All the time it's do this, don't do that," I shouted, giving voice to all the tiny earthquakes that had been shaking inside me for months. "I'm fed up with you in my house all the time, sneering at me and everything I do. Sitting on my bed with your trainers on when I've told you a million times to take—"

"You are so annoying!" Dean exclaimed, clutching at his hair so it stood up in little tufts. "How did you get to be so annoying? Sometimes I can't bear to be in the same room as you."

"No one's asking you to stay!" I hissed pointedly. "The door's over there." And as I flung out my arm to gesture at the exit, I caught the side of Dean's face with my fingertips. Not hard—but the contact was, well, a little forceful.

Dean grabbed my hand. "That wasn't very nice." He wrapped his fingers around mine and smirked when I tried to snatch them away.

"It was an accident," I insisted. "Lemme go!"

He lowered his head so our eyes could meet. "Let's get one thing straight, Molly," Dean purred. "This is my band as much as it is yours. I made everything happen and just be grateful that I'm taking you along for the ride."

Our faces were so close that I could stare straight into the stormy gray depths of his eyes, which were fixed unwaveringly on me. I stopped tugging to free myself and let my hand limply lie in Dean's grip. And as he kept gazing right into me, I suddenly became aware of the heat coming from his body and the slightly accelerated sound of his breathing and the way that his mouth was millimeters away from mine. All I had to do was pucker my lips slightly and we'd be kiss—As soon as I began to think it I pulled myself away from Dean, who stood there, breathing hard, his eyes glittering.

"Come here," he murmured in a soft, insidious voice, but I was turning away and running nervous finger through a pile of revision notes on my desk.

"You should go," I announced shakily, pretending that he hadn't just said what he'd said, because I wasn't quite sure I could process the last five minutes. There was silence, and when I turned round, I was looking at an empty room.

That scene with Dean made our relationship worse and better in equal amounts. Worse, because every time we were together the air around us seemed to buzz with tension. Things had been said (mainly by me, I admit) and I couldn't just unsay them. They lay between us like a lumpy pillow—not doing anybody any harm but getting in the way all the same. Better, because the ferocity of those ten minutes in my room had scared us into being polite and civil and all those other qualities that are so necessary when you're in a band with each other. Fortunately, this new cordial behavior didn't have a chance to get put to the test, as I did the school thing while the others went to London to prepare for our big London showcase gig, which was happening during half term.

The parents conceded, after much foot stamping and door slamming on my part, that I could take two days out from my hectic A-level revision schedule to "do your pop stuff." So a week later, I was sitting in a corner of Paul's office surrounded by my English literature notes while Paul drew things on a flip chart.

"So, after Glastonbury, you have a week of rehearsals, which takes us to here," Paul was saying, pointing to the relevant date with his magic marker. "And then a week's residency at The Lizard Lounge. There should be a bit of press to do between then and now, but we'll sort that out as it comes. The Thursday gig is going ahead as we planned it."

"Is there a guest list?" Jane wanted to know.

"You can have three people each."

I smiled. Three people! The only people I knew who'd actually want to come were sitting round the glass-topped table in this office.

"Molly," Paul said inquiringly, catching me unawares. "Something you wanted to add?"

Everyone, including Dougie, our publicist, and Blue, Paul's assistant, turned to look at me.

I looked down at my notepad where I'd written: *Form and content are inseparable, but we must separate them in order to criticize.* I shook my head. "Nah, I was just thinking . . . about, y'know, nothing."

Paul came round the desk to rest a hand on my shoulder. "Oh, poor Molly," he drawled. "You've got so much to think about with these exams. It's such a pity we couldn't persuade your parents to put them on hold for a little while."

"Molly's family are really into the importance of getting a good education," Tara rushed to explain, and I felt Paul's fingers flex slightly against me.

"It's all right, Paul, really it is," I said. "The exams'll be over soon and I'll be one hundred-and-ten percent committed to The Hormones. I'll be Commitment Girl, honest."

Paul's hand moved from my shoulder to the top of my head, which he patted gently. "I know. I just don't want my little star to get all stressed out before her big show."

I could see Dean and Jane exchange a look, which involved much smirking and rolling of eyes.

"So, Molly shouldn't worry about the press, then," Dean said smoothly. "Maybe I could do the interviews, just to help out?"

"Great idea! Then we can put Molly out there bit by bit. Launch her with an exclusive piece, front cover, of course. Really hype her unavailability," enthused Doug, before I could yelp my objections. I'd been practicing my interview technique since forever.

Dean just sent a vengeful glare in my direction—I fielded it with a demure smile.

The record company was putting us up in a hotel. Well, it was really more of a travel lodge opposite Euston Station. Though my room wasn't big enough to swing a cat in—maybe a small hamster—it was so cool. (Whenever I went on holiday with Mum and Dad, we went camping. I had to share a tent with Joss, who'd always wake me up in the middle of the night because he wanted to go for a pee and was too frightened to head for the nearest bushes on his own.) My room was done in tasteful shades of beige and brown, and the free toiletries had already brought Tara out in a nasty rash—but I could lie in bed and watch television. There was no one to stick their head round the door and try to test me on irregular French verbs or ask if I wanted some chamomile tea.

That night, Paul took us out to dinner to a Chinese restaurant, where they put bowls of water with little flowers in them on the table between courses so we could rinse our hands. It was *so* sophisticated. But *Paul* was so sophisticated. When Tara insisted that she didn't like spicy food and was happy having some plain rice, he ordered six different dishes for her to try. And when she decided that, yes, she did rather like the crispy duck and the chicken satay, he gave her this radiant smile that made my stomach dip. OK, it was only much later that we realized that those six extra dishes and the travel lodge bill and even the guitar strings were all going to be paid for by us. But at the time we felt like we'd traveled between dimensions and arrived in some alternate universe where social outcasts were treated like visiting royalty.

"You all right, Molly?" Paul asked, sliding into the seat next to mine, when Jane slipped to the loo.

I nodded and took another gulp of the white wine he'd ordered for us. The only alcohol I was allowed near at home was this disgusting pear concoction that Dad made in the garden shed. Or the Bacardi Breezers that Jane would buy me from the offie.

"I'm fine," I said. "Thanks for all this—dinner and taking us out."

Paul waved a dismissive hand. "It's nothing compared to the kind of life you're going to have." He looked at me pointedly and then nudged his chair closed to me. "You're going to be famous, Molly. Rock star famous. You're going to stand on a stage night after night and hear people screaming your name. You'll have hordes of journalists begging for the privilege of asking you what you eat for breakfast. Every boy in the country is going to dream about you and every girl is going to dream about *being* you."

His voice was this seductive throb that drowned out the clatter of cutlery and the hum of conversation. His blue eyes were fixed steadily on the blush I knew was sweeping over my face, down my neck, and straight to the tips of my toes. His hand snaked out to where mine rested on the table, and he lightly traced my knuckles with his finger. "Are you ready for that, Molly?"

I glanced across the table to Dean and Jane, who were berating T about something, and Tara, who was tentatively sniffing a forkful of something that looked like bean sprouts. Then I turned back to Paul, who was watching me with an amused smile on his face.

"I don't know," I said truthfully. "I don't know if any of us are ready."

"It's just as well then that I'm here to help you, isn't it?" Paul replied, and he tightened his grip on my hand before letting go and asking if anyone wanted another drink.

I could feel the sweat beading down my back as I leaned over the toilet bowl and dry heaved again. I was just thinking that it was another false alarm, when the chicken sandwich I'd had for lunch decided to make a bid for freedom and hurled its way up my throat and out of my mouth with all the velocity of a high-speed train.

"Do you think that's everything now?" Dean said from somewhere behind me as I rested my forehead on the rim of the loo and tried not to inhale any of the fumes.

I groped for the flush with my hand and pulled it, before getting shakily to my feet and stumbling toward the others who were gathered at the doorway.

"Are you OK?" asked Jane in a concerned voice, putting her arm round me and leading me over to a sagging sofa in the corner of the dressing room. "Shall I get Paul? Do you want some water?"

"Oh, God, I don't think I can do this," I whimpered, slumping forward so my head was practically touching my knees.

"You look awful," commented Dean, ignoring my remark. "Jane, she needs more makeup."

"No, I really don't think I can go onstage," I protested. "I just feel really, really sick with nerves."

"You've been all right when we've played before," Jane said, appearing with my makeup bag in her hand. She knelt down in front of me and inspected my face critically, before grimacing and waving her hand in front of her nose. "You should brush your teeth, Moll. It would make you feel better, plus your breath is all pukey and gross."

I collapsed back against the cushions with a groan, but Dean wasn't having any of it.

"Five minutes and then we're on," he stated grimly, before stalking off in the direction of the stage.

I rubbed a hand over my tummy and pouted. "I can't go on," I groaned, and waved a feeble hand at Jane, who'd started dabbing at my face with a powder puff. "I'm terrified."

"But you don't get stage fright," Jane said.

"Well, I've got it now," I snapped. "We've only played four gigs before, and now it's all important and people are expecting us to do well."

"Molly's right," Tara agreed from the corner, where she was copying down the set list. "It was easier when we were expected to screw up."

"We're not going to screw up," Jane insisted firmly, like she was channeling her inner Dean. "Now go and brush your teeth and get your arse on stage."

I didn't feel any better as I walked on stage. The lights were hot and so bright that I couldn't actually see the audience, but I could feel their eyes on me.

I picked up my guitar and crouched down to play a few chords, partly to make sure it was tuned in but really to ignore the urgent messages that my alimentary canal was sending my brain.

The others were standing in position and looking aggressive. Dean was adamant that we shouldn't look wussy before launching into a hyper-performance.

But that night my performance didn't want to launch itself. Dean nodded his head, and the backing tape music died down and away we went. Except I didn't. Tonight I couldn't lose myself in the music, I was too aware of the scary music business people that had been standing at the bar when I made my way to the dressing room. And my sixties polyester dress kept riding up my thighs every time I moved. My bottle of water tasted of the dry ice that was swirling around us. It was all I could do to remember what song we were meant to be playing, let alone think of something witty to say to the audience in the way of midset banter. But worse than that, I was having technical problems. There must have been a loose connection on my amp because my guitar kept cutting out. By the time we got the last but one song, "Toxic," Dean was glaring at me and there were squeals of feedback coming from my amp every time I stepped on my effects pedal.

I tried to look all moody and unconcerned, like I was the coolest thing in the world. But then someone shouted, "Learn to tune your guitar already!" and it freaked me out. The audience was there to support us and cheer and whoop delightedly—they were so *not* meant to heckle. I stumbled over the last lines of the song and finished the refrain to more feedback and a slow handclap from the crowd. It was like a really bad dream I'd had once—but at least I was wearing more than Scooby Doo knickers this time.

Our last song, "Magic Marker Love," was meant to be this storming, stomping, take no prisoners rock-out. As we blasted into it, Jane had her foot up on her amp and Dean had dropped to his knees and then started rolling about on the stage. He was such a show-off. I stood rooted to the spot, listening to my guitar making this god-awful racket, when something cold and wet drenched me. A nanosecond later an empty plastic beaker richocheted off the neck of my guitar. Some evil git had thrown his drink over me!

I looked round to see if anyone had noticed, but Dean was writhing about the floor and Jane was jumping up and down, and I felt this white hot rush of rage reach up inside me. I wrenched my guitar off, nearly strangling myself on the strap in the process, hurled it across the stage, and flounced off in such a way that the following week's *NME* would call me a "rock 'n 'roll baby diva." Whatever. I was mad and wet and not amused when the two security guards at the dressing-room door pretended to scramble out of my way like I was a bullmastiff who should be put down under the Dangerous Dogs Act. I collapsed on to the sagging sofa and waited for the others to finish the set. It was just as well we didn't do encores—Dean thought it was more punk rock to leave the audience "gagging for us."

"Jesus, what is your bloody damage?" Dean bellowed at me before he'd even got through the door. "What was with the prima donna routine?"

I pouted and said nothing.

"You spent most of the set standing there like you were made of reinforced concrete, and you obviously didn't tune up properly, and what about all the stuff you were—"

"Here's your guitar," said Tara, plopping down beside me and putting the recalcitrant instrument on my lap. "I don't think it's broken."

"Yeah, despite the fact that you threw it violently across the stage," shouted Dean, abandoning one rant so he could start another immediately. "God, we can't afford for you to screw up! This is serious."

"Oh, give it a rest, Dean," Jane snapped, opening a can of lager. "Molly had a bad gig. It's not the end of the world."

"Yes, it is!" Dean practically screamed, before turning on his heel and stomping out the door.

Jane took a long pull at her drink and then looked at me, and

I looked at her, and then Tara nudged me with her elbow, and I couldn't help it. I started smirking, and Jane shook her head and began to giggle, and when Paul walked into the dressing room a minute later, the three of us were clutching our sides and shaking with laughter.

"The gig wasn't that awful," he exclaimed. "No need to cry."

"Not crying. Happy tears," Jane spluttered.

"No, not happy tears. Tears of hysteria," I managed to get out, and started giggling manically again.

Paul smoothed a hand down his polka-dot shirt and stood tapping a Gucci-shod foot while he waited for us to calm down.

"Got that out of your systems, have you?" he wanted to know, when our cackling had dissipated to nothing more than a few choked chuckles.

We nodded, and I noticed him looking at my legs where my stupid polyester dress had ridden up again. I tugged at the hem of my skirt, and he hurriedly glanced away.

"You need to come and say hello to a few people," he murmured distantly. "Some journalists and a couple of producers and someone from the Belgian office."

I struggled out of the depths of the sofa while Jane put the lager can to her lips again and finished it off in one gulp.

Paul shepherded us back into the club with one hand resting on the small of my back as he guided us through the crowd, toward the bar. As we met a succession of people who didn't actually listen to a word any of us said but rather talked at us, I noticed Dean slouched against the back wall talking to a skanky-looking girl in leather trousers and a ripped vest. When I turned back a minute later to raise my drink at him in a silent gesture of apology for making him so mad, he was curled around her with his tongue making an urgent investigation of her back molars. I wondered why the sight of someone I loathed getting way friendly with a random girl made my stomach hurt.

And then it was back to Southport, to my other, not-so-glamorous, more organic life. My stop/start pop career was stuck on the "stop" setting for three months of A-level revision, while the others kicked their heels in London and waited for me to be done with the book learning so we could reboard the rock 'n' roll train at "Almost Famous" station. Or something.

It was like none of it had happened. My head was stuffed full of French vocab and theories about Monet's use of light. Being in a band was becoming a dim and distant memory. I went from classroom to bedroom and the color-coded revision schedule my dad had made me, and back to classroom again. The only brief respite from school and veggie casseroles was my first big interview for *The Hot List*, which took place in a cafe in Southport, while Dougie sat next to me and disappeared in time for me to get all tongue-tied over the questions about sex and my own particular non-experience of it.

The day that I sat my final exam, was the day the mag went on sale with my face peering anxiously out from the shelves with the headline: IS THIS THE SEXIEST VIRGIN IN BRITAIN? slapped across my midriff.

Inside it was even worse.

Reprinted by kind permission of *The Hot List*

A ROCK STAR WITH A LEVELS

BY EVERETT PARKES

SHE SITS OPPOSITE ME IN THE CAFE THAT TIME FORGOT. Outside, the sea blusters against the cliffs, and inside, a skinny girl with hair the colour of over-ripe strawberries twists sugar packets through nervous fingers and sighs every time I ask a question.

We all hate child prodigies, don't we? Those brainiac kids who pass their Maths GCSE while the rest of us are still figuring out potty training, but 17-year-old ('Can't you just say that I'm nearly 18?') Molly Montgomery is a genius of another kind. Although she learnt how to play a guitar less than a year ago and wrote her first song on the back of her French grammar book, she's already being compared to everyone from Ruby X to Courtney Love. If they wrote songs about art students and being abducted by aliens who look like Ryan Phillippe, that is.

'People always bang on about how songs have to say something,' Molly says, in a voice as soft as a whisper. 'But I think a song will say something when it's good and ready.'

She does this a lot. Answering questions with a clever, arch response. And it's only when I play the tape back on the train that I realize she's given nothing away. Well, almost nothing.

There seems to be some weird tension between you and Dean when you're on stage, I remark as the press officer is despatched to the counter for another Diet Coke, which Molly seems to run on.

Another sigh. 'I don't know why you'd think that,' she finally says after a pause that seems to last several millennia. 'Dean and I are friends.'

Where did you meet? I pursue, and she suddenly looks up and fixes me with an icy, blue glare. 'At a gig. It's all there in the record company biography.'

I try to go for a more direct approach. Are you a couple?

She almost snorts Diet Coke all over the table top. 'As if!' And then she collects herself. 'We're just friends. It would get way too complicated if we started dating.'

So you've thought about dating then?

'I didn't say that,' Molly whispers at me, and goes back to tracing patterns in a spilt pile of salt with her fingertips.

But you *are* seeing someone. Your songs are all about love, aren't they?

Those pouty lips twist. 'I'm not . . . I don't. My songs are just stories. Songs don't have to be real. Like, Eminem writes songs that are stories, and no one asks him if he killed his wife and tossed her body into a river.'

But your songs are quite sexy. I quote a line from 'I Can See My Life from Here,' which stayed in my head after their last gig with its awkward sensuality:

I can see my life from here and it only starts
when you're near
And I can see my world from here and you're
the one who makes it,
Only you can make it.

Yet another sigh. 'That's not about sex,' she hisses and casts a frantic look round for the press officer, who's shooting the breeze with the short-order cook. "How could you think that? It's about this girl and this boy, and she takes him to this hill ... It's so not about sex. I'm 17, for goodness sake.'

17-year-olds have sex.

'Well, I don't ... I mean ... Oh God, that's it. That's the headline isn't it? SHE DOESN'T HAVE SEX. Like I'm some kind of great, big, not-having-sex freak.'

I grin. I can't help it, but it's enough for her to realise that she's just put her trainer-clad feet (pink Nike Air Maxes, very two years ago, if you were wondering) into that beautiful, little rosebud mouth.

• • •

The interview went on and on like that. As if I was this sexy, mysterious girl who spent all her time putting her unfulfilled lust into writing songs. Paul went mad when Dougie told him what I'd said, but when it was printed and the press and radio picked up on it, he didn't seem to mind so much. And after that whenever anyone wrote anything about me, the word *virgin* always appeared in the first sentence along with the phrase "reluctant sex symbol," which was a joke considering that I'd never even kissed a boy. Not that surprising when a mere six months ago I was still being called Molly Mong by the more Neanderthal boys in my class. And it was even more ironic that later on when . . . *stuff* had happened, they were still banging on about my virginity.

But anyway, before that, like I said, there were A levels and the day after the underwhelming experience that was my last exam. Then I was back in my usual seat on the London train. This time my bags were packed for an indefinite stay, and I had a Tupperware container with a lentil bake in it, because Mum reckoned that anything you bought from the buffet car was bound to be injected with huge doses of salmonella. I chucked the lentil bake down the loo and bought a burger for lunch.

Soon I was struggling past the ticket barrier with two holdalls, my guitar case, and my practice amp. Blue, Paul's assistant, was waiting for me with a tall, shaven-headed man wearing a kilt and tapping his feet impatiently.

"Hi, Molly," Blue chirped brightly. "How did the exams go? Great? Great! Hope you're not too tired 'cause, *hey, shopping*. This is Rocky. Rocky this is Molly. Rocky's coming shopping with us.

Isn't that great? Great! You've got your own stylist. Hurrah! Paul was really pissed off about your trainers being two years out of date in that interview. Boy! Said you were a fashion disaster about to happen. Didn't like that retro thing you were wearing at the last gig either. So, y'know, do I hear *stylist*?"

I'd forgotten how much Blue liked to talk. No one else could get so much as a syllable in when she was around. But I was too furious about Paul thinking that I was completely fashion backward to care. I glared at Rocky (bet that *wasn't* the name on his birth certificate), who glared back at me before running a desultory eye over my jeans and Beavers T-shirt that I'd nicked from one of Joss's little girl mates.

"No tits," he sniffed. "S'pose we can fake 'em."

"Ex*cuse* me!" I began, but Blue was grabbing one of my bags and marching off to the taxi rank. Rocky gave me one last condescending glance and flounced off after Blue, and I heaved up the rest of my luggage and scurried to catch up.

"I don't need a stylist," I stated firmly, once we were in the cab and heading in the direction of Notting Hill.

"Need is putting it mildly, sweetie," Rocky snapped. "If I have to look at that T-shirt much longer, I might just throw myself into the oncoming traffic."

"It's meant to be ironic," I informed him tartly.

"Irony is dead."

"Blue . . ." I turned to her for help, but she was busy, manically texting on her phone. "I don't need help dressing myself. I'm not spending loads of money on crappy clothes just because they're by some overrated designer."

Blue sent her message. "Dean said you would be like this,"

she said teasingly. "It's gonna be cool. No! It's gonna be fun. Great? Great!"

Actually it was a lot like shopping with my mum. Except she wouldn't have been so eager to get me into the kind of hooker-wear that Rocky thought would give me a bit of sophistication. Between Blue's selective hearing and Rocky's threats, I was cajoled into outfits that should have had a parental advisory sticker slapped on them.

When I met the others later at a belated gathering to celebrate our record deal, I was wearing a push-up bra and a shiny black dress that made my breasts look like two puppies trying to break free from a bin liner.

T shook his dreads for a few moments, in a manner which suggested that he was in some distress, before blurting out, "Look at them!" It's never good when T manages to speak.

Jane gave him a none-too-gentle poke in the ribs. "Hello! Molly's standing right in front of you," she squawked, coming to the rescue. But then she noticed my uncomfortably upthrust bosom.

"Hey, you didn't happen to have a boob job, did ya?"

"No," I growled, folding my arms over my chest and scowling. "Could we find something else to talk about? Like, say, oooh that stupid stylist Paul hired."

Jane, Tara, and T looked at me blankly in a way that roughly translated as: "Stylist? What stylist? We don't have a stylist."

They were obviously all conspiring against me, and so with a frustrated little scream, I turned on my heel and stalked off.

• • •

It was a horrible party. I mean, as parties go it was good because the music was cool and there were these cute mini fish fingers (or goujons, whatever). But it was meant to be a party for us, and we didn't know anybody there.

I kept trying to talk to Paul about how sneaky and underhand it had been to hire Rocky and discuss my alleged fashion backwardness with everyone who wasn't me. But each time I opened my mouth, he suddenly saw someone in the crowd that "you simply have to meet—and be polite, they're very important."

All the people that I simply had to meet made eye contact with my nipples and talked about radio play in Japan and how the Internet was killing the record companies and blah blah blah breaking America and blah blah blah contractual negotiations. At some stage someone put a glass of champagne in my hand and I sipped it willingly because it meant I didn't have to talk. The faster I sipped, the faster a waiter would come and top it up. It was like quantum physics or something. The level in my glass never dropped and it wasn't until Paul asked me if I was OK, that I realized I was standing there, swaying gently from side to side.

"I'm fine," I beamed at him. "I like champagne 'cause it tastes nice and it has bubbles."

He smiled at me absently. "Cool. Isn't that Jane over there?"

I turned my head slowly. "Yup, it's Jane." I looked more closely. "It's Jane with her tongue shoved down the throat of the lead singer of Bikini Dust, if we're going to get technical about it."

Paul ran a hand through his hair and narrowed his eyes. "How much have you had to dr—"

"Which is just freaky," I continued, completely cutting through whatever Paul had been about to say. "'Cause she said that his band sucked and that he had stupid lyrics, and anyway he's going out with this girl who works at the Arts Center and she . . . What?"

Paul had his hand between my shoulder blades and was firmly pushing me away. "God, Molly! You're pissed," he said with a sharp edge to his voice that I hadn't heard before. "I want you to go and drink some water right away and if anyone talks to you, for god's sake look interested."

"But—"

The push became a definite shove. "NOW!"

I didn't go and drink some water because I was mad at Paul for the whole Rocky incident and, besides, I liked the way the champagne took the top layer of my senses and left me feeling slightly numb. Numb was good. It meant I didn't have to think about stuff. It also meant that my spatial awareness wasn't all it could be, and as I cannoned off the side of a table, somebody gripped my arms to steady me.

"Oh, it's you," said Dean in a displeased voice.

I hadn't seen or spoken to Dean since the gig. In fact, the last time I'd seen him he'd been sucking face with the skank. You'd think it would be difficult to be in a band with someone you hadn't spoken to in three months, but it's surprising how well you can communicate via the medium of Jane's text messages.

"And . . . you," I said brilliantly. "Hey, Dean, how you doing? Did they get a stylist for you too, 'cause that would explain your terrible choice of shirts?"

There was nothing wrong with Dean's blue short-sleeved bowling shirt, despite the fact that it had the name "Hank" embroidered on the pocket, but it seemed petty to let a little thing like the truth get in the way of a good insult.

Dean's lips curled, and I knew a moment of sweet success before his eyes suddenly drifted downward and then almost popped out of their sockets.

I folded my arms across my chest for the twenty-third time that evening. "You're such a pervert!" I hissed. "Stop looking at my breasts."

"I can't help it," he drawled with a snarky grin. "You look . . . amazing. In a not good way. I mean, you don't look like you. Did you get your tits done?"

I tried to punch him but almost ended up overbalancing. Hand-to-eye coordination was getting to be a bit of a problem. Dean grabbed my upper arms again, keeping a firm grip on them as I lurched to one side with the force of his momentum.

"Don't *talk* about them either," I snapped. But Dean was too busy taking in my hair, which had been teased into these stupid little twists, and my face, which had the entire contents of Blue's makeup bag slapped over it.

"No, don't tell me. Let me guess," Dean said with a smirk. "Tonight, Matthew, I'm going to be a five-dollar crack whore."

I tried to struggle out of his grasp, but without much energy Dean managed to evade my efforts to break free and made a tutting noise.

"I hate you," I huffed. "I hate you *so* much. You suck."

Dean seemed distracted by my mouth, which was slathered with half a tube of Strumpet lip gloss.

"Yeah, hate you too," he said absently.

"No, I *really* hate you," I insisted, still flailing about. "Stop looking at me like that."

Dean smirked again. "How am I looking at you, Moll?" he purred. And when his voice dipped down low like that, it made my nerve endings *itch* in a way that wasn't entirely unpleasant.

"Like how you're looking at me now," I said with a breathy whisper. And I was just thinking, "Wow, why did I make my voice go like that?" When Dean suddenly bent his head and licked my bottom lip!

"Ewwww," I squeaked. "What are you doing, you freak?"

And Dean smiled, and then he was swooping down and his lips were pressed against mine, teasing them open with the tip of his tongue, and he wasn't so much holding me upright but holding me against him. I opened my mouth so he could do devastating things inside it. He tasted like beer and chocolate. Then my fingers were curled into his hair and my back was against a wall, and he was cupping my face with his hands so gently that—

"What the hell are you two doing?"

Dean disengaged his mouth from mine long enough to say something very rude and Anglo-Saxon. Then he was nibbling on my lower lip again while I gazed up at him and wondered whether it was his kisses or the club decor that were making me see sparkly lights in front of my eyes.

To my eternal shame, I actually whimpered when Dean's warm body was suddenly wrenched away from where it had been pressed against me. "Huh? No fair," I mewled, and then promptly shut up when I saw Paul looming over me with a face like a very pissed-off thunderstorm.

"What did I just tell you?" he demanded.

I shrugged. "Can't remember," I mumbled. "I want Dean back. Go 'way."

Dean said something to Paul that I couldn't quite hear but made Paul's face look even more thundery and stormy. Then Dean wasn't there anymore, and Paul was frog-marching me across the club. He yanked me through a door, up some stairs, into an office, and pushed me down into a chair.

I sank back into its leather depths as Paul stalked over to a fridge in the corner of the room, took out a huge bottle of water, and walked back to thrust it at me.

"Drink," he ordered.

I unscrewed the top and took a couple of baby sips to show willing, while Paul grabbed a chair, placed it wrong way round in front of me, and straddled it. Then he just sat and glared at me, and I suddenly became very interested in drinking as much of the water as I could. This went on for what seemed like forever but could only have been a couple of minutes. It was like a Quaker prayer meeting or a Mexican standoff. I couldn't decide which.

"Is this the bit where you tell me you're disappointed in me?" I asked in the end, with a lot more bravado than my quivering internal organs would have me believe.

Paul looked at me coldly. "Yeah, but you missed out the part where I'm furious with you too."

I could feel icy feet walking up and down my spine. Paul was acting way too headmasterly for my liking, and I had a nasty feeling that he was about to give me a week's detention and a letter for my parents.

"What does all this mean to you?" he asked after another uncomfortable silence.

"What does *what* mean to me?" I said sullenly.

Paul gestured with his hand. "Being in a band, being on the cover of magazines, being famous. All of it."

I wanted to say something amazingly articulate and clever that would stop Paul in his tracks and make him realize that I was an icon in training. But I was just a seventeen-year-old girl who'd had too much to drink and been caught kissing someone who I didn't even like. So I just pulled a face. "Dunno."

Paul scraped his chair nearer so his face was inches away from mine and I could feel the little puffs of warm air when he spoke. "I don't think you realize that you're on the edge of something so fantastic that it's going to change your life forever," he said, taking my hand and squeezing it gently. "And I know it's overwhelming and a little bit frightening, but that's why I'm here. My job is to take care of you, guide you, know what's best for you. Will you let me do that, Molly?"

I looked up from where I'd been contemplating the rim of the bottle to find Paul gazing deep into my eyes. He was so close, I could see the little flecks of gold in his blue eyes. And then I gave my head a little shake.

"I get that, Paul, I really do. But I feel, like, I don't know, like I'm being taken over," I struggled to get the words out, to make sense of what didn't make sense. "It's all so fast. And everyone keeps telling me that I'm going to be famous and that I'm brilliant, but then they keep expecting me to change and become someone that I'm not. Do you know what I mean?"

Paul stroked the underside of my wrist, just where my pulse was, with the tip of his thumb. His touch was hypnotic and calming.

"Look, I don't want to change you, nobody does," he said soothingly. "But the other part of my job is to make sure that you realize your potential. That you understand what a special girl you are."

"Dad says that you're only interested in my potential to make you a lot of money," I blurted out, thinking back to the argument we'd had when I'd refused to think about going to university. Paul's face clouded over and he tightened his grip on my wrist, before continuing with the rhythmic stroking.

"You can't expect your parents to understand," Paul said in a tight voice. "They don't have a clue about you. They still treat you like a little kid."

I nodded my head in agreement. He'd got that right.

Paul leaned forward to rest his hands on my shoulders, so we were practically nose to nose. My whole body seemed to be aware of him, and I couldn't decide whether this invasion of my personal space was delicious or just squicking the hell out of me.

"You have to trust that I know what's best for you," he said softly. "Will you do that for me, Molly? Will you trust me?"

It was an unfair question. It was really unfair. I wanted to yell at him about the lyrics and Rocky and getting some respect. Those were the things that seemed important. Not being mad famous. But then there was the new guitar and the expensive meals and all the money that was being thrown at my two-years-out-of-date trainer-clad feet and it seemed churlish to be so ungrateful. So I just nodded again, and when Paul raised his eyebrows questioningly, I said with as much conviction as I could muster, "OK, I'll trust you."

Paul patted my shoulders. "Thanks. That means a lot to me, 'cause I have to say something and I know you're not going to like it . . ."

I felt the fear begin in the pit of my stomach. "Oh, God, what? Do you want me to pose in a bikini for *FHM*?"

Paul gave a throaty little chuckle. "Nothing like that." He laughed. Then there was a pause. "I don't know what's going on with you Dean—" I opened my mouth to deny everything, but Paul held up his hand. "No, I don't want to know," he continued. "But it's got to stop. Interband relationships don't work. They're bad. They'll screw up you and the group."

"It was just a kiss," I protested. "It didn't mean anything."

"Look, I don't need to know the details," Paul insisted. "But all I know is that couples in bands self-destruct and take everything down with them."

"But, I, y'know . . ." God, I couldn't say a word to defend myself or disagree, because kissing Dean had been stupid and strange and I hadn't even begun to fathom out the reasons why it had happened. I was still opening and shutting my mouth in an unattractive manner, when Paul suddenly pushed his chair back and got to his feet.

"Remember, you're going to trust me to know what's best for you, right?" he repeated.

And he did know what was best for me. Saw me in a way that nobody else did. Plucked me from obscurity. Rescued me from my parents and boring university lectures and working in Best Buys.

"Right," I said firmly. "You're right. I know you're right. I'm on message about Dean, you don't have to worry."

Paul gave me one of his rare and brilliant smiles. "Good girl," he said softly. "You should tidy yourself up a bit before you reemerge." And then he was out the door.

I wandered over to the mirror on the far wall, thinking hard about the conversation Paul and I had just had when I stopped short.

I looked at the reflection in horror. Jesus! The Strumpet lip gloss was smeared all over the lower half of my face. I hated Dean.

Sometime later that night, when I was back in the Euston travel lodge with my head halfway down the toilet bowl (which was getting to be an old look for me), I suddenly realized that something had changed. I was no longer a kiss virgin. I'd been kissed. Thoroughly, passionately, and definitely kissed. And even though I'd always imagined that my first kiss would be in a flowery meadow with a sensitive, feminist boy who'd hold my hand tenderly, I was glad that it had finally happened. I just wish it hadn't happened with Dean.

The next morning when I stumbled down to breakfast with a pounding head and sore throat, Dean and Jane were already in the dining room mainlining black coffee. It was a dilemma. I desperately wanted to get the 411 on Jane's smooch with Mr. Bikini Dust, but I didn't know how I could face Dean. I was just about to duck out of the door and head for the nearest Starbucks when Jane caught sight of me and beckoned with an impatient hand.

I sidled over to their table and stood there, shifting my weight from foot to foot, until Dean looked up from his fried breakfast and gave me a tired smile. "You sitting down or just jiggling?" he inquired with a slight bite to his voice.

I sat and then because it was too much effort to keep it upright, rested my head on the table. "Coffee, please," I managed to squeak as a waitress appeared at my side with a percolator jug and then shut my eyes. OK, I felt rank, but it was also a great way not to have to deal with anything.

"I was so wasted last night," Jane confessed. "God, you'll never guess who I pulled?"

"Bikini Dust," I mumbled. "Sucking face."

"Aw, our little girl's almost managing full sentences," cooed Jane. "She's getting all growed up."

"Talking hurts," I tried to explain, and attempted to maneuver the coffee cup to my mouth without lifting my head.

"So what did you two get up to?" Jane asked.

My head shot up at the same time as Dean snapped, "Nothing. We didn't get up to anything."

"No need to be so touchy," Jane said in a hurt voice.

I simultaneously patted her hand and sent Dean one of my patented death stares.

"I don't remember a thing about last night," I stated firmly. "'Cept the champagne and then my stomach violently rejecting the champagne. I probably made a fool of myself. I always do really stupid, idiotic, completely out-of-character things when I get drunk," I added pointedly. Then I winced as Dean noisily scraped his chair back and stalked out of the dining room without so much as a "bye."

"He can be a jerk sometimes," Jane commented darkly.

"Yeah, he's Mr. Jerk McJerk. So, you and Bikini Dust? You know he's got a girlfriend, right?"

Jane stretched her arms luxuriously. "Just the way I like 'em. Keeps them from getting all slushy and talking about feelings," she said breezily.

I rested my head on the table again and listened to Jane pontificate at great length about Mr. Bikini Dust's lack of technique, while she stroked my hair. And tried not to think about Dean.

Not thinking about Dean was hard over the next couple of months as we did the festival circuit. It was great to do Glastonbury without having to stay in a family tent with Joss and Mum and Dad, who were always intent on dragging me off to the healing field and making the same lame jokes about how it might heal "your hormones." Oh, excuse me while I die of laughing.

This year, we were staying in this semi-luxurious Winnebago that used to belong to a heavy metal band and was decked out with the purple shag pile and black-and-chrome fittings. "All the better to seduce young groupies with," Dean had said when he'd seen the mirrors on the ceiling, and I'd made a complete fool of myself by asking why they were there.

I did meet up with the parents at Glastonbury, but I wished I hadn't. Blue was meant to have organized backstage passes for them, but she'd forgotten. It wasn't until I got an angry text message—Dad had finally caved in and got himself a mobile, only to keep tabs on me—from them that I realized. "Molly! Names not on list. PLEASE CALL AT ONCE! You promised Joss he could meet Slipknot. Please remember family responsibilities." My dad can even be annoying with only 160 characters to play with. Paul sorted it out in the end, but that meant I had him glaring at me, Dad glaring at me and muttering things about "feckless music business types" under his breath, and Mum trying to bond with the band and banging on about how Glastonbury wasn't like it used to be. And when they told me off for the liberal use of swear words in *Teen Angst*. Paul was right, they did still treat me like a little kid.

After Glastonbury, the rest of the festivals were a doddle. It was slightly odd to perform in broad daylight, but we went down really well. My throat got hoarse from singing and being accosted by girls who wanted to tell me how much they liked the band and was Dean seeing someone?

Dean was *so* seeing someone. The skank, or Hobiscuit, as Jane had christened her, was now a permanent fixture in our entourage, which also consisted of tour manager, roadies, Dougie, and Blue. Paul popped up every now and again to make the others sign pieces of paper and tell us we were sounding "really tight."

Anyway, Hobiscuit, who claimed her name was Sandrine (but I saw her passport when we went to Belgium to play Roskilde and she was actually christened Sandra), pretty much ignored us. Though this might have been because her mouth was permanently attached to either a bottle of alcohol or whatever bit of Dean she could reach. Not that I was bitter or anything. I mean, it solved the whole Dean problem, but at the same time it made me mad that he'd kissed me when he'd obviously been doing a damn sight more than kissing Hobiscuit too.

Live Review

THE HORMONES DO READING

I was so psyched to see The Hormones. I'd heard their song 'Hello Kitty Speedboat' on the radio and bought their EP when it came out **BUT THEY NEVER PLAY LIVE!**

This is probably because Molly's still at skool. Tho she's just left. So when I knew they were playing the second stage on the Saturday at Reading, I bagged my place in the front row really early. The first few bands were really crap, and I needed a wee really badly, but The Hormones were on next!

First the drummer and the keyboard girl came on. Then Dean was standing **RIGHT IN FRONT OF ME.** He's *so* dreamy. He had a Jon Spencer Blues Explosion T-shirt on and a pair of weird checked wool trousers — but they looked really kewl on him. Jane was standing next 2 him with her aqua green bass. She had on this tiny black dress and fishnets and combat boots and she was all like, 'Yeah, Reading rocks!' and stuck her fist in the air and Dean was laughing at her.

Molly was the last to come on. It was so cute, she had this little Emily Strange bag that she set down on the stage and pulled out a bottle of water. She was wearing this flow-ery top and jeans that were a little too long and a little bit too big and flowery flip-flops. Oh and she had a flower in her hair too. She looked so kewl!

Then she stepped up to the mic and in this tiny voice said, 'You're there, we're here. We are The Hormones and we've come to steal your children!'

THEY ROCKED! THEIR SONGS ARE SO KICKASS!!! Molly introduced them and said funny things and her and Jane were jumping up and down and Dean was standing there looking moody. He is so foxy.

Then this boy got on stage and tried to kiss Molly, and she looked horrified and the roadies threw him back into the audience. But then everyone was trying to get on stage and Molly made the roadies let all the girls who made it sit at the side so they didn't get hurt. I was going to go up too but I had a really short skirt on and I didn't want people to see my knickers!

Afterwards I was looking for Lyric and Cherrybomb and I saw Molly and Jane queuing up at a crêpe stall like normal people!!! I was dead nervous but I went up to them and said how great they were and would they do an interview. Jane was a bit stuck-up and said how they had a press officer but Molly was so kewl. She kept saying, 'But why do you want to interview us? We're not really famous.' And I was all like, 'Yeah, you're kewl.' And she smiled and looked really pleased. And then **SHE GAVE ME HER E-MAIL ADDRESS** and said that I could send her some questions 'cause she wrote better than she talked. So watch this space!

I ♥ THE HORMONES.

Suddenly it was September, and we were being shipped off to the country to record our album. My A-level results had come through and were much better than anyone could have anticipated (don't ask me how), which had resulted in another screaming match with the parents about how I was throwing my life away, so I was pleased to escape. There's only so much "Dear, please tell Molly to pass the low-sodium salt" that a girl can stand.

I'd always thought that recording studios were either dingy little places below kebab shops, just like the place where we'd recorded the EP, or palatial suites in big London skyscrapers. But Nemesis Studios was based in an ivy-strewn manor house outside of Bath that was so ridiculously picturesque it looked like it should have been the location for some big BBC costume drama. This kinda explained why it cost five hundred quid for each of the fifty days we stayed there, even though it was owned by our record company. But Paul assured us that this was something for the accountants to worry about, and at the mention of the word *accountant* I tuned out the rest of the sentence.

I won't bore you with the details of the actual recording, though the three days that it took to mic up the drums almost destroyed my will to live. I just remember Dean and T fiddling with all the knobs on the desk and getting told off by Paul, Dickon, the engineer, and Stuart, our producer.

But I remember the hours that Jane and Tara and me would spend sitting on the patio steps that led from the control room to the gardens, drinking Diet Coke and rehearsing our Brit Award acceptance speeches. And I remember Maggie, the housekeeper, making us whatever we wanted to eat, which was usually pizza and chips, and the endless games of Ping-Pong we played while Paul, Dean, and Stuart listened to the playbacks and told the rest of us to disappear.

If we finished a session early, we'd stroll down to the village pub, and Jane would have too much to drink and challenge the locals to a game of snooker and I'd sit and talk to Stuart. Stuart had worked with Ruby X when she was just starting out, and he'd tell me stories about how she'd had no money and had to walk for two hours every day to get to the studio but always wore really expensive French perfume. And how once she'd been unhappy with her vocals and thrown a mic stand at the control desk. It got to the stage where Paul would groan every time I said to Stuart, "Tell me another story about Ruby," and tease me about getting even more ideas on how to behave like a prima donna.

Paul was different out of London. More relaxed. He'd abandoned his suits for jeans and expensive-looking shirts, and he didn't *twitch* as much as he usually did. Dean, Hobiscuit, and Tara would eventually have to take a drunk Jane back to Nemesis, and Paul would sit and talk to me about his plans for my world domination, which went as follows:

1. Build up cult following
2. Release album
3. Build up bigger grass roots following through extensive touring
4. Album goes platinum
5. Break America
6. Release second album
7. Find suitable film vehicle for me

"What happens next?" I'd ask, and he'd laugh and say that I'd probably go solo and marry a footballer.

So there were fun times. There were also times that were . . . less fun. Like the rows between me and Dean that would suddenly erupt out of nowhere and have everyone assuming crash positions or running for the nearest emergency exit.

Our biggest row happened on a rainy Wednesday afternoon when we were cooped up in the control room listening to T record the same thumpety-thump-thump over and over again.

"Have you got a name for the album yet?" Paul asked me as I perched on the edge of the control desk with my feet up on the arm of his chair. I was amusing myself by moving my toes nearer and nearer to Paul's arm and watching him try really hard not to flinch away. It wasn't as if my feet were dirty or icky or anything, I'd won a Little Miss Pretty Toes competition once at the annual

Southport Carnival, after all. But Paul was not appreciating the beauty of my freshly painted tootsies one little bit.

"Me and Jane thought it would be really funny to call it *Greatest Hits Volume One*," I suggested, waggling my toes and being rewarded by the way Paul tried to imperceptibly inch away from them.

My toe torture was interrupted by a snort from Dean, who was sitting on the sofa with Hobiscuit in his lap.

"That's stupid," he said dismissively. "People will think it's a singles compilation."

"No, they won't," Jane chimed in. "It's, like, ironic."

"It's *moronic*," Dean huffed. And Hobiscuit giggled and stroked her hand down his chest.

I narrowed my eyes. Hobiscuit's continued presence was getting on everyone's nerves, especially when she kept hinting that she wanted to do backing vocals. Why the hell had I let Dean kiss me? And, way more importantly, why the hell had I kissed him back?

"You got any better ideas?" I demanded, the unwelcome memories giving my voice a vicious edge to it that I didn't altogether like.

"Actually I do, I think it should be called *Uneasy Listening*."

"No, don't tell me," I gasped. "Gosh, it's a clever play on words of the popular musical term 'easy listening.' Bor-ing!"

"It's not your band, Molly," Dean said aggressively, pushing the Hobiscuit gently off his lap and getting to his feet. "It should be a joint decision."

"Jane likes *Greatest Hits Volume One*," I insisted. "And Tara does too, don't you?" I added, shooting her a warning glare.

"I like both of them," Tara said diplomatically.

It was always like this. Dean and I would fight to get Jane on our side, while T and Tara would refuse to get drawn in.

"There's no way that the album is going to be called *Greatest Hits*," Dean growled. "No way."

"Look, most of the songs on it are mine," I hissed. "You just helped with some of the fiddly bits. I wrote the words, I did most of the tunes, so you can just shut up."

"Yeah, but I get joint writer credit," Dean said between gritted teeth, his fists clenching.

I frowned. That didn't sound right, but I wasn't going to let a minor detail stop me from getting my own way. "Maybe we should call the album *My Name's Dean and I'm a Dick, Stop Me and Ask Me How*," I said so cattily that even Jane looked shocked.

"You are such a bitch," snarled Dean, and took a step toward me. He looked so angry that, with a frightened squeak, I slid off the desk and rushed behind Paul's chair so there was something between me and Dean. He was giving off the vibe of a boy who would dearly love to throttle the life out of me.

"Or if you don't like that one, we could call it *Lives and Loves of a Hobiscuit*," I continued, even braver now that Paul was acting as a human shield. "Or *Groupies: A User's Guide*. Or, or, or *Dean Sucks* . . ."

"You are a nasty, spiteful, frustrated, can't-get-a-boyfriend, oooh-I'm-so-confused, scrawny little cow!"

"And you're a conceited, up-himself tart who sucks face with stupid skanks because you can't—"

"God, how I loathe you." The quiet venom in Dean's voice stopped me midsentence, and something about the sincerity in the way he said it made the breath hitch in my throat. Dean and

I screamed and shouted at each other at least twice a day, but those five words, softly and savagely spoken, wounded me far deeper than all the insults that got hurled on a daily basis.

"WILL BOTH OF YOU SHUT THE HELL UP!" Paul suddenly shouted, leaping to his feet. "Just shut up. You are both a pair of spoiled little kids who should be thanking their lucky stars at how privileged they are, instead of slagging each other off and upsetting everyone else."

Paul glared at each of us in turn while I stood there, shaking with the ferocity of the argument. I could feel my bottom lip wobbling and tears pricking at the back of my eyelids as Paul gave me a particularly withering look. And then I burst into tears because everything just seemed so out of control and whacked. Like a line had been crossed and there could be no going back.

Paul's expression softened instantly. "C'mon, Molly, there's no need to cry," he said in a calmer voice. "All bands have rows. It's part of the creative process."

That just made me cry harder. Was my whole life going to be spent having stand-up rows with Dean in the hope that it would make me a successful artist?

"I'm sorry," I spluttered between sobs. I turned to Dean. "I was being a bitch, I apologize."

I wiped a hand across my eyes while Dean stood there with his arms folded, looking completely underwhelmed at my olive branch.

"Well, I'm not sorry," he finally said in that scary soft tone again. "I'm sick to death of the sight of you, the stupid songs you write and the way everyone thinks you're some sweet, shy little genius when in actual fact you're a greedy, grasping . . ."

I didn't wait to hear the rest of the sentence. I fled the room with Tara calling after me, "Molly! Molly! Are you OK?"

I ended up storming out of the house and going for a long, rain-soaked walk and practicing more insults to use on Dean at a later date. I moped and mowed about the rain-sodden country lanes like one of those crazy women in novels by the Brontë sisters. Except I wasn't wearing a bonnet and didn't have to eke out an existence as a governess to a brooding man with a mad wife locked away in his attic. My life was *far* worse than that. And if I caught pneumonia from tearing about in a torrential downpour without a coat on, it would be all Dean's fault.

Meanwhile back at Nemesis, according to Tara, Stuart was dispatched to find me before I *did* catch pneumonia or something equally damaging to my vocal cords. And I missed the rewarding spectacle of Paul blowing all his designer-clothed cool by completely laying into Dean and telling him to stop picking on me. He'd also said that I was sensitive and high-strung because I was an artiste and finding it hard to cope with all the attention, and that Dean should be helping me deal with it.

The upshot of all this was that Jane and Tara starting calling me "The Artiste Formerly Known as Molly" every time they reckoned I was showing signs of diva-esque behavior, like refusing to relinquish control of the TV remote. And when I got back from rampaging through soggy hedgerows and was curled up on my bed looking like I'd just emerged from the nearest swamp, there was a knock on the door, and Dean edged into the room and hovered over me.

"What now?" I asked wearily, not even bothering to look up.

Dean sat down on the edge of the bed and I resisted the urge to cringe away from him.

"Paul said I should sort things out with you," he said with a slight edge to his voice.

"If you're sorry because, y'know, *you're* sorry—fine," I mumbled. "But if you're sorry because Paul thinks you should be, then forget it."

"We can't go on like this, can we?" Dean said flatly. "The fact is you hated me from the first moment we met."

I sat up and shoved the pillows behind my back. "Yeah, well you've always made it your mission to be as confrontational as possible." I sighed heavily. "Look, I wish we were the best of friends, but we're not. So let's just agree on that and try to get on with each other."

Dean shrugged. "S'pose I can do that." He sounded hurt. "So do you want an apology or not then?"

I had to really restrain myself from rolling my eyes. "It's up to you," I managed to say without raising my volume level. "If you *are* sorry."

He shifted on the bed so his weight pressing down on the mattress moved me nearer to him. "You wanna kiss and make up then," Dean said with a small smile.

God, there was so much *mess* in the small space between us on the bed.

"No kissing," I said darkly. "Just an agreement that we'll save the name-calling for when the other one's out of the room."

Dean gave a little chuckle. "OK, deal. You coming down for dinner? Maggie's making something that isn't pizza."

I ran my fingers through a wet strand of hair. "In a minute." I made to scramble off the bed, but Dean's hand shot out and grabbed my forearm, and he leaned in so he was right in my face. "Hey! You're invading my personal space!" I yelped, panicked.

"I know you're all bent out of shape about me kissing you," Dean said, his breath caressing my earlobe. "But it's not gonna happen again, Molly. Sandrine's just about all I can handle."

And then, with a smug smile because he knew he'd got the last word in, he let go of my arm and sauntered out of the room, while I wished that he'd fall down the stairs and break every bone in his snarky, smug body.

And you want to know what the really funny thing was? In the end the record company decided to eponymously title the album *The Hormones* by The Hormones.

There were a few more weeks of "putting down tracks, man" and the icky (with added ickiness) horror that was recording my vocals and listening to my lispy voice echo back on the playback. In the end I wrote signs that said SHOUTY NOT POUTY and stuck them all over the walls, because Dean reckoned I sounded "like Kylie's wussier little sister" and that my vocals should be "way down in the mix"—but he knew he was pushing his luck. And all my buttons. Besides, Paul would never have let him get away with it.

So finally we were back in London, but not staying at the Euston travel lodge anymore. The others were renting a flat in Camden, and I was living with Aunt Pauline and Uncle Lesley in Finchley, which wasn't even a tiny bit rock 'n' roll—probably because my lodgings had been parentally approved.

"I am not having my daughter living with four other equally feckless and irresponsible kids," my dad had announced, when he'd turned up with the rest of my luggage and plonked himself down in Paul's office and refused to move.

"But Dad, I'm almost eighteen now . . ." I'd begun to whine, only to be quelled by Father's Filthy Look Number Twenty-Five.

"I'm doing this for your own good, Molly," he'd gone on firmly, while I winced inwardly and wished that he didn't actually go out in public wearing jumbo cords and Birkenstocks.

"You always say that when you're about to make me do something that I don't want to," I grumped. "And you're making a complete show of me."

Paul sat behind his desk, fiddling nervously with a paperweight. Things were never good when he and my dad were sharing the same airspace. Paul pretended to be all respectful and conciliatory, but I could tell he thought that my paternal signifier was a tree-hugging tosser. He never said anything like that to me, but he made enough arch comments in my hearing about hippies for me to get the general drift.

"And you also said that you'd send us a copy of the contract for our lawyer to look over," Dad said, giving Paul a flinty-eyed look. "You haven't."

Paul attempted to look surprised. "Oh. That got sent out days ago. Maybe it's been lost in the post? So, anyway, about Molly's living arrangements. This flat has got twenty-four-hour security and a fitted kitchen—"

"Molly's going to be staying with her aunt and uncle," announced Dad firmly. "She can be in central London in twenty-five minutes on the Northern Line, and we'll know she's being properly looked after."

Paul simply smiled blandly. "I know you're finding Molly's

new life rather hard to adjust to, Mr Montgomery, but I think we both have Molly's best interests at heart."

But Dad had just sniffed and despite my low-level hissy fitting and Paul's smooth assurances, he wouldn't budge.

I'd never have admitted it to anyone, but I quite liked living with Aunt Pauline. Uncle Lesley was never there because he spent most of his time selling double glazing. But Pauline made me a cooked breakfast every day, did all my washing for me, and mended every single one of my charity-shop clothes (which always seemed to end up with holes, broken zips, buttons missing, and ripped seams). "Oooh, you are hard on your clothes, Molly," she'd sigh, and then ask me if I'd met Robbie Williams yet. Plus, she never told Dad when I didn't have enough money for a taxi home and crashed in Tara's bed without ringing first. Even though she was Dad's only sister, I know that they'd had a big falling out when I was born because she'd been scandalized at their decision to put me on a meat-free diet. No wonder she was hell-bent on stuffing beef casseroles and roast chicken dinners down my throat now. And if I did stagger in from a gig or a music business party at some unholy hour, she'd get out of bed to make me hot chocolate and ask if I'd had a good time.

I rarely did have a good time, though. As we waded through a ton of interviews and TV appearances in preparation for the release of the album, Paul decided that we should be launched on the London scene. Like we were debutantes or something—but instead of wearing pearls and getting presented at Buckingham Palace, we went to a different gig or party every night. And I mean every night.

"It's important to get your faces known," Paul would say as he shepherded us backstage to have our pictures taken with The Strokes. Or "If you're not being talked about, you're being ignored," he'd say when I overhead him telling some journalist that Tara was secretly dating the actor that she'd just accidentally spilled her drink over.

Every night I'd stand in a different club, clutching a Diet Coke (I'd sworn off alcohol after the Dean kiss-athon) and trying to look animated as people brushed past me. It kinda worried me that I wasn't enjoying myself and swinging from the light fittings. The others were—Dean and Hobiscuit were even described as the new Kurt and Courtney in the *NME*, though Jane knew for a fact that Hobiscuit was best friends with the writer's girlfriend. Dean had taken to wearing this mod suit that he'd had made and dark glasses. He looked really cool in a poseurish, trying-too-hard way. When Hobiscuit wasn't twined around his limbs and was at the bar with a posse of fellow skanks, he'd have a procession of sweet young things throwing themselves at him, while he'd slouch against the nearest vertical surface and look unimpressed. Which just made him seem more alluring, I guess. If you liked that arrogant thing, which I most definitely did not.

Jane, meanwhile, was hurling herself headfirst into the arms of that bitch called fame. She was the ultimate party girl, as if her whole life had been in preparation for going to aftershow ligs. I'd see her from the other side of the room with a bottle of champagne in one hand and a love-struck, skinny-hipped, messy-haired boy in the other. Her smile seemed to come with its own lighting rig, drawing a cluster of admirers around her to hear her diss and discuss the other people on the scene. It was pretty much how she used to behave at Youth Club discos, but the champagne had been a Bacardi Breezer then and the scenesters had ruled our Year Nine common room, not the lower reaches of the charts.

Occasionally, Jane'd look up and see me standing there like a total Betty No-Mates, and then she'd dart to my side, a clutch of hangers-on trailing in her wake like a family of fluffy ducklings. "Oh, sweet Miss Molly," she'd cry. "This is my best girl. Say something funny, Moll." And of course that would be my cue to not be able to think of anything remotely amusing to say. I heard one of Jane's new mates say to Blue, "If that's the voice of our generation, then our generation is royally screwed." Blue had just smiled and blinked her eyes rapidly.

At least Tara and T were bonding. They'd find a tiny corner of a sofa and sit there deep in conversation. I sat next to them once, but they were so busy having this uber-geek rant about how *Star Wars* was a metaphor for organized religion that they didn't even notice me.

I'd always thought that my awkwardness was a thin veil disguising the real me. The me that was funny and could write songs that touched people. The me that would one day find some beautiful, intelligent boy who'd recognize me as his soul mate. The me who was secretly pretty and stylish if only someone would lift the veil and see. But I was beginning to suspect that underneath the awkwardness there was just more awkwardness and not much else. And that would explain why I stood in a room full of people and felt like the loneliest girl in the world.

The Rumour Mill

Next stop was The Lizard Lounge for the pre-tour party for U.S. grunge-meisters **Sludge** and their support act, **The Hormones**. Sludge lead singer, Marco Rodriguez, and Hormones bassist, Jane Fabian, seemed to be crossing the cultural and geographical divides of the two bands very well. Maybe that's why they were rolling around on the floor together. Also getting friendly were Hormones lead guitarist, Dean Speed, and his glamorous girlfriend, Sandrine, who tells me that she's joining the band on tour to provide 'backing vocals and lashings of glamour.' It's just a pity that no one told Hormones singer and reluctant sex symbol, Molly Montgomery, that this was meant to be a celebration. Virginal little Molly (still weeks away from her eighteenth birthday) is getting a reputation on the scene as the moodiest girl in music. Last night was no exception as she sat in the corner scowling and generally acting as if her whole world had turned to broken biscuit. Someone get this girl a personality transplant and fast!

The support slot on the Sludge tour (try saying that ten times fast) was when I realized that we'd divided into three camps. There was Dean and Jane (and the Hobiscuit) acting like proper pop stars and throwing fifty fits when they'd given us the wrong brand of water on our rider (Evian, if you're at all interested). There was T and Tara, with their Game Boys hooked up, trying to annihilate the fire demon in *Pokemon Silver*. And then there was Molly.

It wasn't like I fluttered around being all woe-is-me. I still got on fine with Jane and Tara, and even T would grunt the occasional greeting. Dean and I avoided all but the most basic dialogue like, "Do you want that last Coke?" or "No, I think you'll find that that's *my* effects pedal." It was just that once we'd exhausted talking about last night's performance and tonight's performance and why they kept giving us Highland Spring when we'd stated very clearly that we wanted Evian, there wasn't a whole lot else to talk about.

I'd sit on the tour bus, pretending to read *The Catcher in the Rye* (which Paul had given me when I told him that it had eluded me) and wondering why everyone was having so much fun and I wasn't. There had to be something wrong with me.

I also loathed the members of Sludge with a deep and abiding passion. On the first night of the tour, I was just getting ready for bed when there was a knock on the door. I thought it was the chambermaid with extra pillows, but when I stuck my head out, there was Diego, Sludge's guitarist, brandishing a bottle of Jack Daniel's and asking me if I wanted a nightcap. The next evening, their drummer lunged at me, tongue first, as we chilled out in the hotel bar. And the night after that, Marco Rodriguez himself asked me if I needed a hand in "getting shot of that virginity of yours." And their music blowed.

So we did Doncaster and Derby and Durham, Birmingham, Bristol, and Bath, and had just taken Glasgow by storm when Jane—who'd been nursing a five-day hangover—was suddenly banging on my door at seven in the morning.

I was convinced it was one of Sludge come to woo me, so I ignored the frantic thumping for a while, but eventually I struggled out of bed and stomped over to the door.

"Get lost!" I screamed. "This is getting really annoying."

"Molly, it's me!" came Jane's voice. "You have to let me in, I need to talk to you."

I opened the door slightly and poked my head through the gap. "What?" I inquired crossly. "I was going to have a lie-in. Have you even been to bed yet?"

Jane stood there looking—well, un-Jane-like. She was still wearing the silver minidress she'd had on the night before and seemed lost and fragile, almost as if she'd shrunk a few centimeters during the night. "Oh, Molly," she said, bursting into tears. "I've done something really stupid."

Two hours later, after I insisted that, as well as getting emergency contraception, Jane get herself thoroughly checked out for any icky STDs, we were sitting in the waiting room of the local Family Planning Clinic. It was not the funnest place I've ever been. The nicotine-yellow decor, the hard plastic seats, and a depressing selection of Department of Health posters about the wonders of breast-feeding and how smoking when you were pregnant could be dangerous *and* damage the health of your unborn child weren't really helping the general ambience.

"Won't Paul wonder where we are?" Jane asked for the twentieth time.

I put my arm round her and stroked her back comfortingly. "Nah," I replied nonchalantly. "Left him a note. Said we were going shopping."

Jane smiled faintly and nestled her head against my shoulder. She said something, but it was muffled against my cardigan.

"Hey, I didn't catch that," I said, nudging her gently.

"I said that this sucks."

"Oh, Jane, don't say that. You did something with a guy last night and maybe you shouldn't have, but it's not the end of the world. This stuff happens." I carried on stroking her back and hoped that my words, though they lacked any real experience, sounded sincere.

"Just my luck to cop off with some jerk who can't even remember my name the next morning," Jane started ranting. "And y'know, Molly, life's meant to be great. We're the queens of the scene. World at our feet and all that—so why are we sitting here at nine o'clock on a Monday morning, so I can get a prescription for the morning-after pill."

My stroking hand slowed down a bit and then picked up speed as I tried to desperately think of more comforting words. "I don't know," I ventured. "I think that our lives are only interesting when you read about them in magazines. 'Cause I'm not really enjoying any of it, Jane, you know what I mean?"

Jane sat up and shook my hand away. "I had noticed. I don't know what's wrong with you! You could *try* to enjoy it. There're thousands of girls who'd swap places with you like—that!" She clicked her fingers for emphasis.

"Oh, is that why you have to get drunk every night?" I mumbled, and wished I hadn't said it as soon as the words left my mouth. Jane's head swiveled at a 180-degree angle so she could glare at me.

"It's what pop stars are meant to do," she said in a condescending way. "But I guess you're too busy angsting about not having sex to figure that out."

It was like having a bucket of cold water flung over me. Jane was meant to be my best friend. OK, my best friend who had got me grounded countless times over the last five years and dragged me into endless stupid schemes—usually boy related or elaborate cover-ups to fool parents—and now she'd stuck a knife in my belly and turned it a couple of times for maximum hurt.

"I can't believe you said that," I gasped, my bones stiffening. "How could you say something like that?"

I think it was the catch in my voice, but Jane suddenly sighed and all the fight went out of her.

"Hey, Moll, I'm sorry," she backtracked frantically. "I'm in a crappy mood and I'm taking it out on you."

"Is that what you think of me?" I spluttered. "That I'm some sort of buzz-kill, boring virgin? 'Cause, y'know, if I had a boyfriend I'd be doing it all the time. All the time!"

That hadn't come out the way I'd intended, which might have been why I could see Jane trying very hard not to smile. And failing miserably. Then she started to giggle. "No, you wouldn't. You'd be writing songs about having sex all the time and worrying about your parents finding out."

She was right. But I wasn't going to tell her that. I attempted to keep my mouth all tight and pursed, so I still looked as if I was pissed off—but I could feel the laughter bubbling up inside me.

Jane nudged me with her shoulder. "Hey, is that a grin I see?"

"No," I snapped. "I'm in a mood with you."

"I can definitely see a little smile tugging at the corner of your lips," she insisted, still chuckling.

I pushed at her with my arm. "No you can't." And then I ruined my frosty one-upmanship by laughing.

"I'm pathetic," I told her with a rueful smile. "You're right, I should be living a life of rock 'n' roll excess and instead I'm getting preoccupied with not being able to eat five pieces of fruit and veg every day."

"Really?"

"Yeah, I don't know who sorts out our rider, but they've obviously never even seen an orange," I said, all mock affronted.

"Well, rock 'n' roll excess never looks that good in the morning," Jane sniffed. "I can't believe I shagged Diego."

I nearly choked on my tongue. "Whoa! Rewind! You did it with *Diego*? Ewwww, Jane! What were you thinking?"

Jane shrugged. "I wasn't thinking at all, hence needing a prescription anytime in the next few hours."

I turned to look at her. "Do you fancy him? I mean, Diego . . ."

She sat forward, arms hugging her knees. "I had too much to drink, and we were in the bar and I didn't want to go to bed too early 'cause—hello! Never going to happen. And he asked me back to his room for a nightcap and like you said, stuff happens."

I didn't know what to say. Whether I should be sympathetic or have a go at her for not using a condom to protect herself against all the revolting diseases that Diego had probably picked up from shagging a different groupie every night. But then Jane sighed.

"Stuff seems to be happening to me an awful lot. Don't get me wrong, I love being in a band and all the attention that I get, but sometimes I wish everything was simpler. Like it was before."

She was still Jane, still my bad-girl best friend and I loved her. So I put my arms round her and wished that I could gather her up and take her to a place where we were both anywhere but where we were.

Then a woman in a white coat called out Jane's name, and

when she emerged fifteen minutes later, she was a little bit paler than when she went in.

Jane muttered something about how stupid it was to take a pill that was probably going to make her vomit, and I took her limp hand and we walked to the exit.

"I have to take another pill tonight, before we go on stage," Jane said, looking at a piece of paper she'd been given. "Will you remind me?"

"Yeah, course I will."

"Molly, I'm sorry about what I said about you being a virgin," Jane suddenly choked out, and pulled me into a shop doorway. "I know I joke about it, but I really respect you for waiting for the right boy. And . . . and . . . and that stupid bet that Sludge have about you, I'm so proud of you for seeing through them."

I frowned. "Huh?"

Jane pulled a face, squinting in the bright sunlight. "Somebody told you, right? Dean would've told you . . ."

"Told me what?" I asked with a slight feeling of dread.

"I can't believe no one told you," Jane muttered, rolling her eyes. Seeing the complete lack of getting-a-clueness on my face, made her clutch my hand tighter. "OK, there's no point in getting upset about this because it's completely stupid and idiotic and you know what boys in bands—"

"Just tell me!"

"Sludge are running a book on who can get you into bed first. There's, um, a five-hundred-quid pot for the winner. I thought you knew. I mean, we all knew. I really thought one of the others would have . . . Moll, you all right?"

I leaned against the shop window and tried to process the information Jane was spewing out.

"Oh, my God," I managed to say. "You didn't happen to do a huge bunch of drugs last night too, did ya?"

"I know you're upset, but we'll laugh about this soon. One day. Many years from now. We'll go: 'Ha ha, remember that time when Sludge tried to shag you for five hundred quid?' Honestly."

"How? What? Who? I mean . . ." My cognitive thought processes seemed to have taken the morning off.

"Help me out here, Molly. Complete sentences would be good," Jane said, still trying for light humor and sounding as if she was auditioning for a role in a Greek tragedy.

I pushed myself away from the window and stood up straight so the whirling, white-hot rush of anger could come out of my mouth.

"That bunch of no-brain, think-with-their-dicks, crappy, arrogant, tuneless, no-brain . . . Think they can treat me like some panting, desperate-for-a-shag . . . I'm telling Paul. I'm complaining to their manager. I'm gonna have them for sexual harassment."

"OK, just calm down," Jane warned me as I started walking very fast in the direction of the hotel. Sprinting, actually, if we're going to get technical about it.

"Calm down? Calm down? I'm going to throttle someone," I shrieked. "I don't care who. Not fussy. I'm so over this "reluctant sex symbol" stuff. So, I'm a virgin? So, I've only been kissed once? No one would even think it was worth talking about if we were still stuck in Southport going to lame discos and—"

"You kissed someone?" Jane asked wonderingly, running to catch up with me. "You never told me, you cow. Who was it?"

I came to a shuddering halt. "Nobody," I said quickly. "Just somebody."

Jane had an inquisitive look in her eye, like she was going to take the matter further.

"That's not important now," I reminded her. "I'm going to . . . actually, I don't know what I'm going to do, but it won't be pretty, and it will contain language that some people may find offensive."

Unfortunately when I exploded into the hotel foyer, Sludge were still safely tucked up in their beds.

I tore through the lobby and into the restaurant where Paul was finishing a leisurely breakfast, which was ruined by me standing over him and ranting while Jane stood to one side wringing her hands.

"What are you going to do about it?" I yelled when I came to the end of my tirade.

Paul looked bemused. "Didn't really catch most of that. Why are Sludge giving you five hundred quid?"

I gave a tiny scream of frustration. "Why does nobody listen to me? They have a five hundred quid bet that one of them's going to *do it* with me! Go and tell them off! Now!"

Paul shook his head and poured some coffee into his cup. "I don't get paid enough for this," he said with a sigh. "Jane, get lost. Molly, sit down."

Jane exited stage left with indecent haste, and I threw myself at the nearest chair and scowled at Paul.

"It's your own fault," he said unsympathetically. "You should never have said what you said in that interview. I told Dougie to stay with you at all times."

"How is this my fault?" I yelped, my volume level rising. "I suppose you'd prefer it if I was having loads of sex with loads of different people."

I'd kind of forgotten that this was a conversation with Paul. Paul, who didn't "do details. I prefer to see the bigger picture." The subject of my nonexistent sex life was making him squirm, as if his bespoke suit was made of something itchy.

"If this reluctant, virginal, sex symbol stuff carries on I'm going to go and do it with the first boy I see," I promised.

"What are you having a tantrum about now?" asked Dean in a bored voice, suddenly popping into view like a scruffily dressed version of the bad fairy.

"Molly's having—"

"Oh, is my personal life now up for public debate?" I hissed. Dean smirked, and Paul gave another sigh that was so heavy it made all the napkins flutter.

"Molly's right," said Paul in a manner that suggested that he though the opposite might be true. "Anyway, aren't you forgetting what day it is?"

"Monday—Edinburgh," Dean and I said in unison.

Paul smiled, obviously pleased that his endless recitation of the tour itinerary hadn't been in vain. "Well, yeah, there is that, but it's your birthday. Molly. You're eighteen. Happy birthday, sweetheart." He leaned over to brush my cheek with his lips. I knew I was blushing bright red at the uncharacteristic gesture of affection. "Tell you what, why don't I take you out for dinner after tonight's show and we can get everything sorted out then?"

I couldn't believe that I'd forgotten my birthday. I lived for my birthday. When I was little, I'd come downstairs every day and chirrup, "Is it my birthday yet?" It's one of the amusing, "Don't kids say the cutest things?" anecdotes that Mum always drags out when she's trying to convince herself that I wasn't always a surly, ungrateful teenager with dyed hair.

The obligatory phone call home was stilted. Mum was wittering on about how they didn't know what to get me anymore and that we'd go shopping when I got home, and then Dad picked up the extension in the study and the temperature dropped a good ten degrees. So *not* Daddy's favorite girl, these days. After some stilted inquiries about my general well-being and the dangers of sex, cigarettes, alcopops, and drugs (in that order), he started going on and on about how the contract still hadn't turned up and insisting that I get Paul to phone him. This then quickly degenerated into an argument about how he was a fascist control freak who hadn't even wished me happy birthday, and I was a rude girl who should be thankful that I had such caring parents.

"Whatever," I snarled, before slamming the phone down.

We had to drive to Edinburgh for the gig that night, and the others (with minimum cooperation from Dean and the Hobiscuit) threw me a surprise party on the tour bus. All of a sudden I felt wanted, and the weeks where I'd felt unwanted seemed to disappear in the air like the smoke from my birthday candles.

Even Sludge were on their best behavior. Somebody (Paul, probably) had said something to them and they sheepishly shuffled up to our end of the bus to apologize and give me a card. When I opened it, a couple of sheets of paper fell onto my lap, and I couldn't stop myself from bursting into hysterical giggles when I saw that they'd repeatedly written in a Bart Simpson blackboard style: *We must not try to shag Molly for money or any other reasons.*

Tara and T had bought me a Game Boy so I could come to share their love of *Pokemon Silver,* and Jane had bought me a vintage pink Mary Quant dress that I wore on stage that night while the audience sang "Happy Birthday" to me.

And if Dean acted as if the whole thing was too boring for words, I decided not to let it bother me. It was just Dean being Dean. But, yeah, it still hurt.

After the show, Jane went to bed early. She said that it was all she could do not to be sick, and that even thinking about food might just finish her off. Dean and Hobiscuit had disappeared to some club that she had been jawing on about all day, which left T and Tara as my dinner dates. But when I looked for them backstage, they'd gone.

"We should wait for T and Tara," I told Paul, who was sitting in our dressing room in yet another immaculate suit. "Your shirt's pink," I added. No one could fault my observational skills.

"We match," he commented silkily, looking at my Mary Quant shift dress. "Look, why don't we leave the restaurant address with the tour manager and they can catch us up. It's just I've made a reservation."

• • •

I'd already had two glasses of champagne (it was my birthday, after all) and scarfed down a starter of mozzarella cheese, and Tara and T still hadn't arrived.

"Maybe we should wait for them before we order the main course," I said to Paul as he refilled my glass.

Paul frowned slightly. "It's ten, I don't think they're coming. I could ring, I guess. Don't run off."

He slipped out of his chair to make the call. While he was gone, I fanned myself with the menu. It was hot and I already felt quite light-headed. I looked around the restaurant, which had four stars from some highfalutin food critic. When we'd walked in, the other diners had given us strange looks—like a sixties minidress and motorcycle boots were in violation of the dress code. I suppose Paul and I made a pretty odd couple. Which was weird, 'cause we weren't really a couple—but then with the matching pinkiness . . .

"You look deep in thought," Paul remarked, settling back in his seat. "They got stuck in traffic and then their cab broke down, so they decided to give it a miss."

My face fell. Great, I get to spend my birthday night with someone who was paid to be nice to me.

"Hey, they said they were both sorry—and, anyway, I'm here. Is my company that boring?" Paul gave me a slightly wounded smile.

"No, don't be silly," I assured him. "It's just you're here, 'cause you have to be . . ."

"Rubbish," Paul said stoutly. "I never do anything that I don't want to. You should know that. Now what do you want to eat?"

Actually it wasn't as hideous as I thought it would be. Paul was on his best, Molly-pleasing behavior and didn't get annoyed with me for taking ages to decide that in the end I just wanted dessert. We talked about art and film and politics. It wasn't like talking to the others or to journalists, who never really hear what you're saying but scribble away in their little notebooks. Paul listened and asked me questions. And when we started talking about music, I told him about Ruby X and wanting to be part of a girl revolution and that all I really wanted was to write songs that made all the other misfit, lonely girls learn to play guitar and form their own bands. "And I hope they do," I said, slightly slurring my words 'cause I'd had too much champagne by now. "I don't even care that they'd be coming up behind me. That doesn't matter. It's all about the music really, isn't it?"

"Yeah, the music," Paul echoed. "Maybe in the future, you could think about starting up your own label."

"That'd be so cool," I squealed, and then sank down in my chair as my high-pitched yowling attracted disapproving glares. "Sorry, I think I'm a little bit tipsy."

"You don't have to apologize," Paul said quickly. "It's your birthday, and besides the people in this place are half dead. You're so alive. That's what I noticed about you the first time we met. How passionate you are when you care about something."

"Really? What else did you notice?" I rested my elbows on the table and cupped my chin in my hands. God, I was drunk.

"That you were shy but you had an inner strength," Paul continued. "And you had that ridiculous wedding dress on, but you still looked cute. I actually thought you and Dean were together."

"As if!" I snorted, and Paul laughed.

"Yeah. He's a little sod, isn't he?" he said lightly. Paul was being so off-message tonight. He'd slipped off his suit jacket and undone the first two buttons of his shirt, and in the candlelight, he looked softer, younger. His dark blond hair was all mussed, and I had a strange impulse to reach across the table to feel if it was as soft as it looked.

"Dean doesn't like me," I told Paul gravely. "Not one little bit."

"Well, he's a fool. He can't see what's right in front of him," Paul commented darkly. "I wouldn't worry about him. You're the star, you're the talent. He's just an above-average guitarist."

"I know the kiss was a mistake, but what really gets me is that he was already seeing the Hobiscuit," I confessed. Paul looked confused. "Y'know? Sandrine—'cept her name's really Sandra. I don't know what he sees in her. Do you think she's hot?"

Paul laughed again. "How much have you had to drink?"

"Probably too much. Hey! We should go to a club! Do you want to go to a club?"

"Maybe . . ." Paul halted for a second. "Oh, before I forget, I need you to sign something, the contract . . ."

I groaned. "God, I had my dad moaning that you hadn't sent it. Can't we do it tomorrow?"

Paul reached inside his jacket and took out an envelope. "It's just there was a mix-up . . . And it really needs to be signed now, and since you're all legal and over the age of consent, it'd save time if you could do it."

"I don't know, shouldn't I get a lawyer to look at it?" I asked worriedly.

Paul waved his hand dismissively. "You don't need to worry about that. Your lawyer drew it up. Do you need a pen?"

I opened the envelope and ran my eye over the document. It was written in legalese and was all "the artist" and "the licensees" and "henceforth." It didn't make a whole lot of sense.

"Molly, they're starting to clear the other tables. We need to go," Paul said urgently. "You just need to sign here and here and here." He pointed to the relevant lines and handed me a pen.

So I signed, because when I wavered, Paul whispered, "Trust me," and the *maître d'* was hovering and waiting to witness my signature. And, like I've already said, you never recognize the big moments when they actually happen. It's only afterward when your life is going down the toilet, that you wish you'd had the foresight to smack your forehead and shout, "Hey, back up there, pal!"

Instead, I got rather unsteadily to my feet and let Paul get my jacket and help me into it, then lead me through an obstacle course of tables and chairs and out into the street where he hailed a cab.

As we drove back to the hotel, Paul was restless. He kept fidgeting with the seat belt and patting his pocket. It made me feel tense, like there was something going on that I couldn't quite fathom out. It made me feel restless too. Then the driver came to a screeching halt as a car suddenly cut in front of us, and I was thrown against Paul. His hand shot out to steady me, and when I stayed slumped against his nice, warm, citrus-smelling chest, he reached up and stroked my hair. "Oh, Molly, you've had too much to drink," he murmured.

"Don't stop, that feels nice," I whimpered when he took his hand away. And the tension was coiling in my stomach, and all I could think about was how good his touch felt on my hair. So I lifted my head and pressed myself against him and kissed him.

His lips were firm and unresisting at first, but I was persistent and pressed my mouth more ardently against his. Paul's hand stopped stroking my hair and slid to the back of my neck to tilt my head so he could deepen the angle of the kiss. The moments seemed to slide by and all there was was his mouth on mine, inside mine . . . Until he shoved me away from him with enough force to send me crashing into the door handle.

"Ow!" I yelped. Then reached for him again.

Paul held his hands out in front of him to ward me off. "Molly! Stop!"

"But I don't want to stop," I mewled. "I knew there was something bet—"

"Please, don't finish that sentence," Paul ordered in a tight voice. "Look, we've both had too much to drink. It was just a kiss between friends. It didn't mean anything."

"It did mean something!" I protested. "Kisses mean something."

"Not this one," Paul insisted, smoothing down his shirt. "I want you to forget about this."

"I—"

"I'm your manager. That's all. And you're a sweet girl and I'm very fond of you but . . ." His voice trailed off and he turned to look out of the window.

We didn't talk for the rest of the journey.

When I woke up the next day, my first thought was that something must have crawled into my mouth during the night and died. Then my brain caught up and I had a slo-mo replay of the cab ride back home. I banged my head against the pillow and then wished I hadn't because it made the thumping ache in my skull hurt a bit more.

I'd thrown myself at Paul. Kissed his face off and been cruelly rejected only moments later. In actual fact, there were other things that had happened that night that should have been worrying, but as I heaved myself out of bed and staggered to the bathroom to clean my teeth three times in quick succession, all I could think about was the pissed-off vibes that Paul's stiff back had managed to emanate all the way back to the hotel.

When I eventually made my pasty-faced entrance twenty minutes later in the lounge where we were assembling for the drive to Aberdeen, Paul acted like nothing had happened. He looked up from his paper, said, "Hi, Molly. Sleep all right?" and then went back to reading the sports page like he'd never had his arms wrapped around me and been nibbling my bottom lip like it was a particularly tasty piece of sushi a few hours before. I didn't know whether to be relieved or furious.

Thankfully after the *Sturm und Drang* of my birthday, the rest of the tour passed by in a blur of soundchecks, midbudget hotels and watching the world pass by from outside the tour bus windows. After Diego-gate (as we referred to the whole Family Planning Clinic incident), Jane had come back to me. I think she'd had the fright of her life. And though she hadn't taken a pledge of temperance, she wasn't drinking so much and preferred to hang out with me at the aftershow parties and bitch about Hobiscuit.

I don't know how, but Dean had found out about our nickname for his girlfriend. And every time he saw me and Jane with our heads together, whispering, he'd stalk over and hiss: "I don't know what you're saying, but it better bloody not be about me and Sandrine." That would be our cue to look all innocent and then laugh like a pair of mentally challenged hyenas as soon as he turned to walk away. It was childish, but gave us immense pleasure.

Jane even managed to persuade me to flirt with Diego as a way of getting our revenge on the love rat. I'd led him out into the loading bay after one of the shows and was letting him slobber all over my neck when Jane suddenly appeared (just like we'd planned) and started screaming, "How can you do this to me? You said our love would last forever!"

In fact, we behaved so badly that Frank, our tour manager, threatened to separate us if we didn't stop hanging out at the back of the bus and and flicking *V*s at unsuspecting motorists.

Being on tour was like living in this hermetically sealed-off bubble that protected you from the real world. There was someone to wake me up, give me money, make sure that I was where I was meant to be at the right time—and there was applause. I could have lived off the applause. It was better than chocolate and puppies and Christmas. To just stand on stage night after night and listen to the roaring of the crowd . . . I wanted to dive right into it and roll around.

But eventually reality has to sink in and when we finished the tour, the itinerary said that we had time off for Christmas. And the itinerary was always to be obeyed, so I took the train back to Southport with two huge bags of dirty laundry and a sinking heart at spending quality time with my parents.

World War III hit just before my pudding on my first night back when I told Dad to stop obsessing about the contract because I'd already signed it. My suspicions that his hippie, tree-hugging persona was just a front were confirmed, because he went ballistic. He banged his fist down so hard on the dinner table that the bowl of organic apple crumble that Mum had just put in front of me upended itself and landed in a heap on the tablecloth. Joss said in one scared gasp, "ThankyouthatwasverynicepleasemayIgetdownnow?" and scarpered.

"How could you be so stupid?" Dad shouted, storming into the kitchen.

"What's the big deal?" I shouted back. "I'm old enough to sign contracts."

"You're barely old enough to blow your own nose," he yelled, coming back into the room with a tea towel. He started patting it into the little pile of spilled crumble but only succeeding in smearing it into the tablecloth. "You've probably signed your entire life away, is what you've done."

"No, I haven't," I snapped. "Paul said—"

"Oh, Paul said . . ." mocked Dad. "When will you realize that your wonderful Paul is only looking after himself? You're just like a can of baked beans to him. He's the human face of a vast corporate conglomerate who want to—"

"I am *not* a can of baked beans," I protested furiously. "I'm an artist. Paul says—"

But before I could finish, Dad threw the tea towel on the table and stomped out of the room.

Mum and I sat there for a second, trying to process what had just happened.

"I don't know what his problem is," I said finally. "Anybody else's parents would be really proud of them, but all he does is put me down."

"We *are* proud of you," Mum insisted. "But we're worried about how fast this is all happening; that you don't appreciate the long-term consequences of what you're getting into."

"What long-term consequences?" I growled. "That at the age of eighteen I get to be successful and influential and independent? You just don't want me to grow up." And despite the way her face fell and her hand reached out to me, I pushed my chair back and flounced out of the room too.

A week later and Dad and I still weren't speaking. I was hanging out a lot at Tara's house with Jane. We'd think about doing Christmas shopping, but instead we'd end up in the cafe by the station drinking cappuccinos and wondering why nothing seemed to have changed. It was like those afternoons when we'd skipped out of school and sat in that exact spot, wishing that our lives were different.

Some things had changed, though. Everyone was home for the holidays, and we were the must-have guests on their Christmas party invitation lists. These were the same people who'd managed to ignore us for the entire seven years that we were at school together. But now my mobile was beeping every five minutes with texted requests to "mt up. B Lvly 2 c u."

In the end we did go to Lizzie Firestone's Christmas party at the golf club. Only because she'd made Jane's life particularly hellish (an incident over a boy that Jane had been snogging every Friday night, without realizing that Lizzie had visitation rights on Saturdays), and Jane wanted to turn up at the party, throw some pop-star fairy dust over the proceedings, and then walk out. And if she got to have Lizzie groveling all over her too, then that would be an added bonus.

The reality was that the three of us sat in the corner so bored that it made our skin itch, while a procession of former schoolmates fell over themselves to ask if we wanted a drink or a dance, and was it true that we were dating various members of Sludge? Jane lapped it all up, and as she knocked back more and more punch, her made-up tales of on-the-road excess became more and more wild. Tara kept bumping my knee with hers and whispering, "I reckon we can leave in another half hour, and if Kevin Brannigan tries to lick my ear again I'm going to hit him."

I sat there folding paper napkins into swans and wondering

why I wasn't enjoying myself. Then I realized that I hadn't really changed at all. Having a minor hit hadn't turned me from a geeky outcast into a witty, sophisticated quip machine. It was just the people around us that were acting like I'd changed, like I was suddenly acceptable. As soon as I had that epiphany, I got to my feet, tugged Jane and Tara up too, and just at the precise moment that Lizzie Firestone tried to hug me and began to gush something, I said in my most biting voice, "This party sucks, let's get out of here and go somewhere more cool." Half an hour later, we were sitting on the wall outside The Soul Place sharing a bag of chips. Rock 'n' roll excess, my arse!

I hadn't seen or heard from Dean the entire time that we'd been home, which wasn't all that surprising as even when we were in the same room we never talked to each other. But the day before we were due back in London, I was mooching around town with a vague idea of off-loading my Christmas book vouchers (my mum's answer to the questions: What do you get for the daughter that a) has everything? and b) isn't talking to her father?) when I bumped into him.

I was in Waterstones looking blankly at the latest releases shelves when someone came up behind me and said, "Hi."

I swiveled round to see Dean standing there, hands shoved into the pockets of his gray fleece, looking at me expectantly. "Hey," I said, and picked up the first book I could put my hands on, staring at the back of the cover intently until Dean went away.

He didn't go away. "What'cha doing, then?" he asked.

"I'm buying books," I replied. The "duh" went unsaid.

"Ok, whatever," Dean said in a slightly hurt voice. And then, "I like your hat. I'll see you."

No one liked my hat. Hell, I didn't even like my hat. It was a green wool monstrosity with earmuffs and a bobble—but my gran had knitted it for me when she was in hospital recovering from chemotherapy to treat the cancer that would kill her a few months later. When I wore it, it made me feel closer to her. Sounds sappy, I know, but for some reason hearing Dean toss in that compliment made everything inside me soften, and I grabbed his arm as he turned to leave.

"Do you want to know why I'm *really* here?" I asked him in a conspiratorial voice.

Dean looked slightly surprised. "What are you doing?" he said suspiciously. "You're not shoplifting, are you? 'Cause Jane told me all . . ."

I was *so* going to kill Jane.

"No," I denied far too quickly. "And, anyway, I was going to pay for those nail varnishes."

His eyes were twinkling. I never knew that Dean's eyes could do anything other than glare at me. I couldn't help but smile.

"I'll have you know that I intend to pay for all my purchaes," I told him in a mock-prissy tone. "But the real reason why I'm here is 'cause I haven't spoken to my dad the whole time I've been home, and I just had to get out. Y'know, have a break from all the not chucking insults at each other?"

Dean nodded understandingly. "I know what you mean," he said feelingly. "'Cause I left home the minute I turned sixteen, and now I'm back in Southport with no bedsit to live in and we only had a short-term lease on the London flat so . . ."

"So?" I prompted.

"No choice but to throw myself on the not-so-tender mercies of my not-so-loving family."

"I hear you," I said. "Families should really come with a no-questions-asked return policy."

Dean smiled at me, eyes still twinkling like he'd borrowed some serious wattage from the Christmas decorations outside. And despite everything, Dean's smile still had the ability to make me feel like I was the most special person on the whole planet. Even though I'd seen that smile used to devastating effect on the Hobiscuit and countless lovestruck little girls, I could feel the corners of my mouth start to turn up, and I was grinning back at him.

"You see anything you like, then?" Dean drawled.

"Huh? What? Oh, you mean the books?" OK, he could stop smiling at me now. "No, not really." I put the book I'd been holding back on the shelf. "Well, I guess I'll see you tomorrow if you're getting the train."

"Yeah. At the station," Dean muttered.

"Right, well . . ."

Dean's gaze was fixed on the bobble on top of my head when he spoke. "I don't suppose you want to go and get a drink, do you?" His tone was hesitant. "I mean, I guess you've got stuff to do . . . So, look, just forget it."

He was already walking out of the shop before the last words left his mouth, and without thinking, I scurried after him and yanked at the back of his jacket.

"Yeah!" I said. Dean slowed to a halt and turned to look at me. "Yeah," I said again. "Let's go and have a drink."

Dean took me to a pub off High Street, full of old men playing dominoes and dribbling into their pints of bitter. But at least it had a proper fire, which we sat next to and drank mulled wine.

It was stilted at first—there was so much we couldn't talk about. But then I told him about Lizzie Firestone's party at the golf club. And Dean told me about him and T gate-crashing the McJob's staff do, and how everyone wanted him to buy them drinks and wouldn't believe that he was on an allowance of £150 a week. We covered the *EastEnders* Christmas special, and whether T and Tara were boinking, and if Lawrence Llewellyn Bowen was a minion of Satan—and by the time they called last orders, we were huddled up close together, a collection of empty glasses on the table.

"I didn't realize it was so late," I exclaimed, fishing for my hat on the floor where it had fallen. "Hope I haven't missed the last bus."

Dean looked at his watch. "We'll probably make it if we run."

We sprinted down the street just in time to see my bus pull away from the stop. Dean tried to get the driver's attention by running alongside it, waving his hands, but the driver obviously thought he was a drunken lunatic and picked up speed.

"Dean, stop! It's no use!" I called out, between giggles. He looked like such a dork.

He leaned over, hands on his knees, trying to get his breath back, as I walked over to him.

I dug around in my bag until I found my purse and starting sorting through the coins. "I've got £1.78 and a couple of book vouchers," I announced. "Can you lend me a tenner for a cab home?"

Dean straighed up and rummaged in his pockets, before pulling out an equally paltry pile of coins. "I've got about three quid. Do you think that will be enough?"

I pulled a face. "Probably not . . . I can walk, it's no big deal."

"You can't walk home on your own," Dean protested. "It's dark and late, and you could get attacked by a homicidal rapist or, y'know, a crazed bunch of Hormones fans."

"You're so much more fun when you've had too much mulled wine," I announced.

Dean looked offended. "Hey, I'm always fun. I'm the very definition of *fun*," he insisted as we started to walk up the road. "Look up *fun* in the dictionary and there's a picture of me."

As we cut across the park, Dean suddenly disappeared into the shadows, leaving me to wander along the path, bleating, "Dean, that's not funny. I'm scared."

"ROAAAAARRR!"

I screamed at the top of my voice as Dean leaped out of the bushes and landed on top of me. My knees buckled and I fell over, with him following me down.

"What did you do that for, you moron?" I yelled, struggling to get out from under his weight. "You nearly gave me a heart attack."

"I was just showing you much fun I am," he said innocently, making no move to get up.

"If I've got grass stains on my jacket, I'm going to kill you," I warned him. "Do you know how hard it is to get suede clean? Especially pink suede . . ."

I stopped my rant halfway through when I became aware of Dean's body pressing against every inch of me, our legs entwined and his face buried in my neck.

"Hey," he whispered, when I finally shut up. He lifted his head so he could look at me properly. In the faint glow of the streetlights, his eyes seemed to gleam as he took in my breathy attempts to stop the impending coronary that I was convinced was imminent.

"Hey, you," I managed to whispered back.

"Can I kiss you?" he asked.

And instead of answering him, I managed to get my hands free and twine them around Dean's neck so I could pull his mouth down to mine. His arms wrapped around me and pulled me even closer as he gently tugged on my bottom lip with his teeth, before planting little butterfly kisses on my mouth, never resting for too long, until I gave a groan of frustration and he sank into my mouth. I don't know how long we lay there, all I was aware of were the curls of his hair between my fingers and the comforting weight of him on top of me and how his kisses made me feel as good as applause.

"No, don't stop," I moaned, when he took his wonderful mouth away from mine.

"Molly, it's really late and we're lying on damp grass," Dean murmured. "I've got to get you home."

Now he mentioned it, my back felt cold and clammy where it had been resting on the wet ground. Dean got to his feet and held out his hand to me. I let him pull me up and wondered how long it would be before we both started coming out with excuses or outright denials about what had just happened. But, instead, Dean kept holding my hand and his other arm rested around my shoulders as we started to walk.

When we got out of the park and started heading up the hill, Dean stopped every few minutes to drag me back into his embrace and kiss the breath out of me. I couldn't even begin to analyze the whys and wherefores of all this frenzied passion, I just didn't want it ever to end.

It took us over an hour to get back to my house, and before I could start dithering about whether to invite Dean in for coffee, he had me backed against the fence and was stroking my left earlobe with the tip of his tongue.

"You should come in," I gasped, 'cause I couldn't bear the thought of him going. "For coffee, and to warm up and stuff . . ."

"You sure?" Dean asked throatily, before attacking my neck with his evil lips that made all rational thought fly out of my head.

We stumbled up the garden path, Dean's arms around my waist, his lips still exploring around my jugular, which made me wonder if he was a vampire in another life. It was hard to concentrate on menial tasks like finding my keys and inserting the right one into the lock, but I finally made it. With the right incentives, I could be very focused.

Dean came up for air as I pushed him into the hall. "You gonna make me coffee, then? I could do with something hot," he asked wolfishly, arching an eyebrow and nudging me with his hip.

"Ssssh," I hissed. "Parents on the premises. Go up to my room and be quiet."

Dean swooped in for a swift, hard kiss, then started tiptoeing up the stairs. I staggered down the hall into the kitchen. As I switched on the kettle and found clean mugs on hot beverage-making autopilot, I tried to give myself a stern talking to: "What are you doing? What are you doing with Dean? Have you gone mad? Right, one coffee and then he has to go. But he does kiss really well. Jesus, Moll! This is Dean. Dean who gets pelvic with the Hobiscuit at regular and frequent intervals. Hmmm, *so* not thinking about Dean and getting pelvic . . ."

I leaned against the counter, lost in my own deeply contradictory thought patterns, until the kettle clicked and I came back to earth.

I toed open the door of my room, set the mugs down on my dressing table, and tried not to look at Dean lounging on my bed like he had every right to be there. At least he'd taken his boots off for once. Then I noticed that he had my old, battered rag doll in his hands.

"I don't think I've been introduced to this lovely little lady." He grinned.

"Dean, don't," I growled. "Put her, I mean it, down."

Dean held Miss Princess Mopsyhead (to give her, her full name) in front of him and made her dance. "Not till you tell me her name."

I muttered something.

"I didn't quite catch that, Molly. Something about a princess . . ."

"Princess Mopsy," I said really quickly, leaving out the Miss and the head and then wishing I'd said her name was Anne or Sue.

"Hello, Princess Mopsy," Dean cooed, and then realized that I was not seeing one shred of funny in the situation. "OK, putting Her Royal Highness down now. Though I could get a fortune for her on eBay."

God, he was back to being all cute and dorkish again, and it was making my skin sing in the most delicious way. I reached over to hand him the coffee mug and then leaned back againt the dressing table.

Dean took a sip, watching me all the time from heavy-lidded eyes. "What you plotting in that busy head of yours?" he wanted to know.

I shrugged and didn't say anything. Couldn't think of anything to say.

"C'mon, Moll, don't go weird on me," Dean crooned. Then he put the mug down, sat up, and was off the bed. Before I could process why that low, husky pitch to his voice made me dig my nails into my palms so hard that I'd still have little half-moon marks embedded there the next day, he stalked toward me, all predatory and sleek. I looked at him. Really looked at him and wondered why I hadn't seen him properly before.

He was long and lanky and had stupid hair that stuck up in tufts and spiky bits all over his head. And his nose was too big, and his mouth was too smirky, and his eyes . . . his eyes . . . his eyes were gray. But right now they were almost black and sweeping over me like he was seeing me for the first time too.

"You've still got your hat on," he said, and reached out to slowly and deliberately pull it off. He took another step toward me, so there was such a tiny gap between us that I could feel the heat of his body stirring up all my molecules and making me feel hot and languid. My hair was in two pigtails, and Dean took out the elastics and started running his fingers through my hair and loosening the plaits. He twisted and stroked my hair, and I leaned back against the dressing table and let him.

When my hair was loose, Dean gathered up two great big handfuls of it and gently tugged me closer.

"Don't," I half moaned, but I was already tilting my head and closing my eyes, because it was easier if I didn't have to look at him.

Dean's tongue was skittering along the roof of my mouth, and I dimly registered the sweep of his hands under my shirt and on my skin. But it wasn't until I suddenly felt the bed underneath me that I realized that Dean had maneuvered me across the room and was lying on top of me.

I pushed at his shoulders until I managed to unglue his mouth from mine, but that only encouraged him to start kissing a path down my neck to the knobbly bits of my collarbone.

"Dean!" I hissed urgently. "What are we doing? Think!"

"We're kissing, we're having fantastic kissing," he muttered. "And we should have done this long ago." His hands were unbuttoning my shirt and tickling every patch of skin that he uncovered, and it was a great way to distract me.

"But it's you and it's me and we don't like each other," I pointed out. "Oh, God, do that again. No, don't!"

With a deep sigh, Dean sat back on his haunches—which just kinda brought his lower half in closer proximity to my lower half.

"I've always liked you, Molly," he purred. "And right now I like you an awful lot. Why do you think we argue so much?"

"'Cause we get on each other's nerves?" I suggested, and wondered when I'd have the chance to pull off his T-shirt.

"Because opposites attract," Dean insisted firmly. "Do you know how long I've wanted to do this?" He ran a caressing hand over my tummy. "Or this?" He bent down and nibbled at the place where his hand had just been. "Or this." His hand crept up—and I grabbed it and linked our fingers together.

"OK, I'm getting a word picture here," I said, but my voice wasn't all stern, it was husky and not very authoritative. "Do you think this is a good idea? God, I can't believe I'm considering what I shouldn't be considering! This is wrong, Dean, it's wrong with added bits of wrongness, and I—" But Dean had long ago discovered a really effective way of silencing my babble by the simple act of kissing the words right out of my mouth.

We were wearing far fewer clothes, and Dean was exploring the back of my knee, the next time I tried to stop the giddy rush of passion.

"W-w-w-what about Sandrine?" I stammered, and Dean muffled his groan against the soft skin of my thigh.

"Molly, are you trying to kill me here?" he asked, his voice slightly sharp.

"Don't know," I answered truthfully, and he half chuckled.

"Are you a virgin? Are you scared? You don't have to be, I'll look after you," he promised. "I'll make it good for you."

I didn't waste any breath denying my very obvious virginity. Even if Dean hadn't discovered my maidenly status from Jane or Tara, my endless stop/start shenanigans had clued him in.

"How are you going to make it good for me?" I heard my voice ask in this half-appalled, half-fascinated whisper. And Dean leaned over me and said, "Like this . . ."

People always talk about how it felt the first time they had sex. Mostly I felt outside of myself, like I was watching me and Dean from somewhere on the ceiling. And I felt like a girl. He was a boy and I was a girl, and after eighteen years I finally got why we were made the way we were. I was vibrantly aware of the difference. Realized why it had to be that way, and it made me feel small and vulnerable.

Afterward I cried, not because I was unhappy and not because I'd enjoyed the kissing way more, but because I was overwhelmed by the enormity of what we'd just done. It made me feel insignificant, part of something I couldn't begin to understand. Dean tucked my head against his shoulder and stroked my tears away with the tips of his fingers and murmured small, soothing bits of nonsense in my ear. "Hey, sweetie, don't cry . . . Shhhh, it's all right, everything is all right," and "Please, Molly, honey, baby, you're going to be OK."

But it wasn't going to be OK. We'd left OK a few hundred kisses back. And when I woke up in the morning, after falling asleep still sobbing in Dean's arms, there was a warm patch of bed where he'd been and then stolen himself away.

I didn't have time to freak out about the sex and the sex and well, the sex that morning. I was too busy trying to pack, remove all incriminating evidence from the night before, and avoid my dad's deafening silence.

Him and Mum drove me to the station, and when we got to the right platform, he wouldn't even say good-bye. Just turned and stared at the chocolate vending machine like it was one of the eight wonders of the modern world. Out of the corner of my eye, I could see Dean talking to T and Jane, and was half scared that he'd detach himself from them, come over, and start making veiled references to deflowering me on my Powerpuff Girl bed linen. It would have been *so* like him. And when I thought about the fact that I had Powerpuff bed linen, I couldn't help but wonder if I was mature enough to even leave the house without my name and address written on my hand in indelible ink. Certainly not mature enough to do what I'd done. . . .

"Molly! Honestly, I don't know where your head is these days." Mum's slightly querulous tone snapped me out of my reverie. "Have you got everything? Ticket, phone, keys . . . ?"

"I'm not—" I began, and she sighed heavily.

"I know, you're not a little kid. Just humor me, OK?" Then she was gathering me up in a Mum-scented hug and it felt nice. Really nice. Made me feel five and carefree again. "We love you and we're proud of you," she murmured in my ear. "Even if one of us is being too bloody silly to show it at the moment."

Dad made a harrumphing noise behind us, and with one last squeeze, Mum let me go. And I am the world's biggest wuss, 'cause I could feel this swollen lump in my throat and the familiar prickle at the back of my eyes.

"I gotta go," I mumbled. "I'll call when I get to Pauline's, yeah?"

Mum gave me a tremulous, watery smile and then turned to Dad with eyes of steel. "Are you going to say good-bye to your only daughter, then, dear? Or are you going to carry on this ridiculous feud knowing full well that she could possibly die in a rail crash?"

Did I mention that I'd inherited the guilt-trip gene from my mother? Oh yeah!

"Bye, then," Dad muttered, not even looking at me, and despite my ownership of Powerpuff Girl bed linen, even I took a moment to ponder who the mature one was.

If the morning after my kiss with Paul was business as usual, then the morning after getting pelvic with Dean was difficult, hideous, awkward, mind-imploding—pick an adjective, any adjective.

He sat across the aisle from the four of us (who'd bagged a table seat) and appeared to be dozing for most of the journey.

But I could see the way his hands were clenched into white-knuckled fists, and the memory of what those hands had done a few hours before made me squirm in my seat.

"You all right, Moll? You're wicked fidgety," Jane observed, watching me wriggle as my helpful and obliging brain provided me with a blow-by-blow replay of the events before, during, and after the sex.

"I need a wee," I yelped, and fled in the direction of the loo.

After I'd washed my face and tried not to breathe in any of the noxious fumes, I unbolted the door to see Dean standing there. OK, he'd seen me naked, but the thought of him being aware of my body's capacity to do things like pee made me blush.

"It's all yours," I said hurriedly, and tried to step past him, but he grabbed my arm.

"We need to talk," he said in a dull voice, and started pulling me into the next carriage, where he pushed me into the nearest seat and then sat down opposite me.

There was a moment's silence and then he opened his mouth.

"If you start that sentence with the words 'about last night', I'll scream," I warned him, and he gave me a tiny smile.

"This is complicated, isn't it?" he said tiredly.

I nodded.

"Look, I'm sorry I left without saying good-bye, but I was worried that your mum would decide to wake you with a cup of one of those disgusting herbal teas and find you—us—in bed together." His voice lowered on the last words, and the intimate way he looked at me made my stomach clench.

"Yeah, I figured it was something like that," I said, though I'd figured no such thing.

"So are you having regrets about it?" Dean wanted to know, being careful not to look me in the eye.

"Not sure," I replied carefully. "Haven't really worked out how I feel about it."

"'Cause I don't," he said fiercely. "Have any regrets that it happened. I'm *glad* that it happened." He leaned forward and put his hand on my knee so I could feel the weight of his palm through the denim. "It was wonderful. You were wonderful."

"Was I?" I squeaked. My blush made a reappearance, and Dean watched in fascination as my face turned a brilliant shade of pink.

"So how are we going to do this?"

"D-d-d-do what? Do it again?" My voice had reached a pitch that was practically only audible to dogs.

Dean gave me a slow, sexy smile, and my blush upgraded from deep pink to bright red. "You offering? Nah, I'm talking about you and me, this thing between us."

"There's an 'us'?" I said wonderingly.

"There was always an 'us.' We just let other things get in the way," Dean explained. "Paul mustn't find out and the others . . . it's too soon. Maybe we should find out what 'us' means and then let them know."

This was going too fast. I wanted to jump up and pull the emergency lever. I hadn't even had time to think about what the sex meant, and Dean was being, like, Mr. Relationship. Mr. *Secret* Relationship. What was up with *that*?

I mean, I did fancy Dean. That, at least, I had to admit now. I wouldn't have ended up bare-arse naked with him otherwise. And that in itself was skewy, 'cause it wasn't until last night that

I'd even realized that I was having lustful feelings toward a boy who I'd previously considered to be a Grade One pain in the butt. And should we just chalk it down to one night of moon and mulled wine-inflicted madness? Could we stand to be together without killing each other? And oh, God, he was looking at me again with that playful smile hovering about his lips and that killer arch of an eyebrow.

"Come here, you," he rasped, and beckoned me with his finger. And I was a fool 'cause I went and sat on his lap and kissed him all the way to Milton Keynes—when I suddenly remembered we'd left the others ages ago, and they were probably about to send out a search party.

January's a great time to release singles by new bands because you don't have to sell many copies to chart. This might explain why our next single "I Can See My Life From Here," went Top Twenty.

We, the Hormones, were a Top Twenty band. That meant appearing on *Top of the Pops* and *CD:UK* and *Later With Jools Holland* because we straddled the divide between bubblegum pop and serious musicianship. People fell over themselves to book us. Or rather book me, because apparently I was "the voice of disenfranchised girlkind" and "had single-handedly spearheaded the return of girls who rock." Whatever.

After *The Hot List* debacle, Dougie had sent me to a media handler who taught me how to give good interviews and talk in sound bites. Jane and I would think of stupid things for me to say in interviews, and we had a score sheet and a point system for anything we could think of that appeared in a headline or a pull quote. In fact, one magazine that had been blacklisted by Paul for publishing a picture of Jane sucking face with someone from *Hollyoaks* (she swore it was dark and that she'd had him confused with someone else) printed a Top Ten of our best quotes:

Reprinted by kind permission of *Siren* magazine

Hormonally Talking

She's not speaking to us, but Molly from The Hormones is speaking to everyone else. And, boy, can this girl give good quote. Here are her ten feistiest moments:

1. 'Atomic Kitten were our main influence. When we heard them on the radio we thought, "My God, we could do so much better."'

2. 'I don't hate all boys. I haven't met all the boys in the world yet.'

3. 'Dean and I aren't dating. In fact, we've actually been married for ten years but the union's only legal in the state of Oklahoma.'

4. 'I'm not a girl, I'm a force of nature.'

5. 'What do my mum and dad think about my success? I don't have parents. I was raised by wolves.'

6. 'If I'd had one happy day at school, The Hormones could never have existed.'

7. 'Interband rivalries are great. I won't rest until I've savagely killed all the members of Westlife.'

8. 'My heroine is Ruby X, because she made me believe that I could change the world with my guitar.'

9. 'You don't have to have sex to be a bad girl.'

10. 'I'm going to give all this up when I'm twenty-one and open a donkey sanctuary.'

When I think back to those months, it was a whirlwind of photo studios and live playbacks. Sitting in studio canteens talking to journalists. Having makeup plastered all over my face and going to the loo to wash most of it off. And tedious rows with Dean and Jane in Paul's office about why I was getting all the attention. "We're meant to be a proper band, not her backing group," one of them would say. "How come Molly gets to do all the interviews and photo shoots?"

Paul would embark on this big speech about how the public were fundamentally stupid and it was easier to present one face, rather than five. And that they got to perform on TV, and maybe Dougie could set up some Internet live chats for them.

That would be my cue to pipe up, "Oh, it would be fun to get Jane and Dean to do interviews with me. We could be, like, a three-headed quote machine."

Paul would stroke his chin in a pensive fashion and promise to think about it. Ten minutes later when I was in a taxi on the way to another one-on-one with some snarky writer, he'd phone me on my mobile and tell me not to be so stupid. "You're the star, we've talked about this," he would growl. "Have you any idea how much time I've spent putting your face out there?"

It was getting harder and harder to remember the pure intentions I'd had when we started the band. I'd lie in bed at night, thinking: girl revolution—check. Writing songs about things that no one else writes songs about—check. Inspiring a generation of loner girls to rise up and storm the citadels of boy rock—check.

But some of those nights, I stayed round at the band flat. Once the others had fallen asleep, I'd carefully get out of Tara's bed (only a direct hit from a nuclear bomb could disturb her slumbers, and even then she'd only momentarily stir) and creep to Dean's room. When I poked my head round his door, he'd always be sitting on the floor, messing about with his guitar, and he'd look up and smile at me. Like, he'd been expecting me. Like he'd missed me. I think it was the smile that did it for me every time.

And later, when we were curled round each other on his narrow, saggy mattress, it was easy to pretend that we were a proper couple. That we didn't have to steal kisses in deserted corridors and dressing rooms when the others weren't around. That we could walk down the street holding hands and talking about the film we'd go and see on Saturday night.

There weren't two people in our relationship. There were five. Six, if I believed Jane's gossip about Sandrine being only temporarily unavailable due to a dancing job that had taken her out of town for a couple of months.

Our conversations were always about the here and now.

"Kiss me," he'd demand, already bending his head and pulling me toward him.

"Are we alone?" I'd ask, turning round to see if we'd been followed, only to have him cup my chin and get me right where he wanted me.

Or in the dark of the night he'd stroke the messy strands of hair away from my face and murmur, "I didn't think it would be like this. That I would feel this."

And I'd run my fingers across his lips and whisper back, "I know."

It made up for the times when the others were with us and Dean would be particularly savage in his criticisms of me. I tried to tell myself that he was just doing it so no one would suspect that we couldn't keep our hands off each other, but when he was ranting and raving about how crap my lyrics were and how I was a power-crazed wanna-be, it made me want to die. Maybe the way the venom poured out so easily was a little too convincing.

So sometimes I felt like I was being torn apart until there was nothing left of me. And other times I felt so top-of-the-world fantastic, I thought my heart would explode into a million glittery pieces.

After the success of "I Can See My Life From Here," Paul and the record company decided to rush-release our album for Valentine's Day. If Dean and I had actually been able to admit to anyone that we were in what could pass for a relationship, we might have spent the day exchanging gifts and kitsch homemade cards, even though we both thought the whole thing was an exercise in crass commercialism. Instead, we spent over an hour rowing about the set list for our performance at the album release party.

"That song sucks, so does that one, and that one, oh yeah and that one too," Dean sneered dismissively at the sound check when I told him what I wanted to play.

"So, basically all the songs that I've written on my own are crap and all the ones that you helped with are fantastic," I translated.

"Better, not fantastic," Dean conceded. "Why do you write so many songs about stuff you watch on TV? Do you have a life?"

I scrutinized his face as he looked down to check the strings on his guitar, searching for some sign that this argument was all part of Dean's clever master plan to fool everyone into thinking that we hated each other. I couldn't see one.

"We should do the singles and the next single and 'Art Boy'— that goes down well live, and so does 'Pick 'n' Mix,'" I said flatly. "And if you want to choose a couple of songs, then fine, suit yourself." I jumped off the stage in time to hear Jane say, "God, what is up with you two? It's like being in a band with my parents before they got divorced."

"I don't want to talk about it," Dean snapped. "She's just getting on my nerves today."

I walked over to the table where I'd dumped my bag and pretended to rummage through it to give myself time to calm down. And just when I thought the day couldn't get any worse, I saw Rocky padding purposefully toward me.

Rocky and I had come to an understanding that I would tolerate his input on my wardrobe (I seemed to need a different outfit for every interview and TV appearance), but that I had final veto on everything. Right down to hair slides. This only happened after he forced me into a pink rubber skirt for our second *TOTP* show, and my mum had phoned Paul up and demanded to know why her only daughter looked like a teenage prostitute.

"Hello, cutie," Rocky greeted me. "You're looking a little peaky. Still not making friends with Mr. Blusher?"

I wasn't in the mood for this. "What do you want?"

"No hello for an old friend? Gosh, Mollykins, you've hardened in the short time it's been my pleasure to know you."

I folded my arms and gave him a look. It was a good look too. Even Dean wouldn't have liked to have been on the end of it.

Rocky merely rolled his eyes dramatically and rustled the bag he was holding. "Found this for you in a vintage shop in Kensington," he explained. "Thought it might do for tonight's little bash. It will photograph well, anyway." Then, with the air of a magician pulling a rabbit out of a hat, he took out a handful of material and held it up so I could see it properly.

It was a black silk, A-line minidress with multicolored geometric patterns all over it and sheer black chiffon sleeves. "My God, who are you and what have you done with Rocky?" I gasped. "This is beautiful." I stroked the fabric with my fingers.

"Well, I thought it would hide the fact that you're built like a fishing rod," Rocky sniped. And then he gazed proudly at the dress. "It is lovely, isn't it? If I could have got my head through the—"

"MOLLY! Get your arse up here now," Dean shouted from the stage.

"*He's* a regular little charmer. Don't know what you see in him," Rocky said tartly.

My heart nearly stopped beating. "I don't see anything in him," I exclaimed. "He's just a colleague. It's just a working relationship. I would never think of him like that!"

Rocky looked bored. "Whatever, princess. Guess he must have something that makes all the little girls scream, though God knows what. I'm going to go and iron this. And please don't wear those horrible Docs with it or I'll come and—"

Rocky never did get to finish his sentence, as Dean suddenly materialized behind me, wedged his hand into my armpit, and hauled me stageward.

After we sound checked, Dean stomped off to sulk somewhere and Jane disappeared after this dodgy bloke who'd been hanging round all afternoon. I hid in the dressing room and spent over an hour fiddling with my makeup and hair and trying to ignore T and Tara, who were picking green things out of a bag of trail mix and wittering on about *Buffy*.

Half an hour later I'd put on my dress, along with a pair of knee-high boots, and was eating the rejected green bits of trail mix and arguing with them about Hello Kitty.

"Hello Kitty is a symbol of feminine suppression," I declared.

"No, she's not, she's just a smug cat. Now, Polly Pocket has a certain charm, I'll grant you," said T, in what was our first ever conversation. (I know this because I made a note of it in my diary.)

"Polly Pocket isn't fit to wait table for Hello Kitty," I hissed, waving my Hello Kitty purse in front of him. "Look at her. Look at how her minimalist form evokes such pathos." I said all this, I really did. "And she has no mouth. She's mute. All her desires are inarticulate."

"We are sad, sad people," Tara suddenly announced. "We've just spent twenty minutes deconstructing Hello Kitty."

"I never knew being a pop star would involve so much hanging about," I sighed.

"When we were making the album, we actually played Ping-Pong for five days. I counted it up," T confessed. "That's a lot of Ping-Pong."

"Do you ever wonder if other people in bands are having more fun than us?" I asked them. "Seriously. 'Cause this is a lot like hanging out in the school common room but without the added threat of double French hanging over my head."

"Well, it beats working the griddle at the McJob," T decided. "But a lot of the time this sucks."

"There are huge amounts of suckage," Tara agreed. "Oh, hey, Dean!"

"Hey, who sucks?" Dean asked, coming into the room and looking at me warily.

"We're compiling a list," I said in a voice that was slightly below freezing. "You should have a look at it, see if you recognize anyone you know."

Dean's face darkened and he turned to T and Tara. "Can you two leave me and Molly alone for a second?"

"They don't have to go," I spat. "They can stay . . ."

"It's all right, we have a . . . thing . . . a thing we have to do," Tara muttered quickly, practically running for the door, with T behind her.

As they disappeared, Dean walked over to the door and shut and locked it. "You mad at me?" he asked, sitting down next to me on the sofa. All dressing rooms came with a brown velour sofa—I think there was a law or something.

"Yeah."

He tried to take my hand, but I snatched it away.

"Look, Moll, what happens with the band and what happens with us are two different things," he began.

I shook my head furiously. "I can't separate the two 'cause I'm not some big schizo freak like you! How can you be all snuggly and 'Ooh, Molly, you're so great' this morning and then tell me that my songs are crap a few hours later?" I shifted myself right down the other end of the settee and turned my head so I wouldn't have to look at him. But then he was squatting down on the floor in front of me, his hands on my knees, his face all hurt. "I don't think I can do this for much longer," I said in a choked voice.

"Hey, hey, Molly. Don't talk like that," Dean said in his sweetest voice—the voice that just made me want to curl myself around him and not let go. "I'm sorry that I've been bitching at you all day. It's just, y'know, when we're alone it's not about the band, it's about you. You being Molly. And if I'm nasty to you, it's only because of the others. If Paul found out, he'd chuck me out of the band."

"No, he wouldn't," I said automatically, though I had a niggling feeling that if it was a choice between Dean or me, then Paul's choice would be decidedly Molly-shaped.

"Look, we'll do the American tour, and then we'll come out as a couple," Dean said persuasively. "We'll be established then. They won't be able to do anything."

"You promise? Because I hate lying to Tara and Jane, and she said that Sandrine—"

"I promise," Dean breathed. "I don't like upsetting you."

His hands slid to my waist and he pulled me toward him so I could bury my face in his neck, which was my preferred comfort zone.

Dean stroked my back. "You look so pretty, Moll," he purred. "Not touching you in public is so hard. So can I have a kiss now?"

With a great effort, I sat up and pouted at him. "Only one kiss, 'cause you've been bad."

We stayed on the sofa, gradually getting more and more horizontal, until someone banged on the door.

"Are you two in there?" said Paul's voice. "Why is the door locked? You're on stage in five minutes."

I stood up and tried to smooth down my dress and my hair, while Dean went to unlock the door.

Paul walked in, looking around suspiciously. "You're very flushed, Molly," he commented archly. "I hope you're not about to go down with something."

"I'm just hot," I muttered, and flapped my hands in front of my face until he left.

"That was close," Dean said as I looked in my makeup bag for my lucky guitar pick. But he still held my hand all the way down the corridor. It was only as we went through the backstage door and saw Paul standing there, tapping his foot impatiently, that he let go.

To be honest, we'd played better. Jane could barely keep time and Tara spilled water over her keyboard. But Dean kept jumping around and backing into me to whisper silly things in my ear, and it made me happy.

I preferred playing to a proper audience and not a crowd of liggers and record company personnel, but no matter how many times I played certain songs, I would feel every word, every chord so intensely. At times like that, it seemed that the song didn't just come from my mouth and my fingers but from my heart too. When we played our last (and my favorite) song, "I Can See My Life From Here," this wash of feeling threatened to drown me. Dean was chiming in on backing vocals, and when I sang the line "There has to be a better life just over this hill," and he echoed the words back to me, I nearly started crying.

I was overdosing on pure emotion after we came off stage. I was so psyched that I ran round the club like the winner in a Miss Congeniality contest, hugging Blue and Dougie, and thanking all the people at the record company who worked with us.

Blue managed to get me to calm down enough to go back on stage for a photo op with a big cake with our faces iced on it and the head of Big Black Records, who'd flown in from LA to meet us (actually he'd had a shareholders' meeting the next day, but it was a good story).

I smiled and smiled, and because the photographers kept telling us to move in closer, Dean put his arm round me and squeezed me gently. "You look so hot," he whispered in my ear. "Sexy hot, not feverish hot."

Later I told myself that it was because I'd got overexcited, but the next moment I'd swiveled round in Dean's arms, tugged his head nearer, and kissed him. For a few seconds he kissed me back, his tongue tracing my lips, but then he pushed me away so violently that I lurched into Jane, who swayed a little bit and then fell off stage. She had such a surprised look on her face that I started laughing. And then I realized that Mr. Big Black was looking at us like we were a troupe of performing chimpanzees. T and Tara seemed dazed, Dean was staring at his shoes, and Paul was stepping up to the mic and saying, "Oh, Molly, she's such a kidder! There's free drinks all night, people, so please make your way to the bar."

I began to edge nearer to Dean but Paul was glaring at us. "You two come with me," he said in the scariest voice I'd ever heard. He practically frog-marched us back down the corridor to the dressing room before locking the door again and proceeding to give us the telling-off to end all telling-offs.

Dean slouched against the door and I sat on the arm of a chair, while Paul paced up and down and shouted. "What the hell is going on? I knew you two were up to something and it stops now! Do you know how many people are counting on you? And you let them down with this infantile behavior! I will not have either one of you jeopardizing the success of the band because you can't keep your hormones in check."

When Paul mentioned the word *hormones*, I actually started giggling. I think it was a nervous reaction, but it just made him more angry. Dean kept giving me these horrified looks as I tried to control myself, but it was no good. I had my hand in my mouth, trying to stifle the laughter, when Paul turned to Dean. "Get lost," he ordered. "I'll talk to you later."

I really didn't want Dean to go, but he shuffled out of the room without a backward glance, while I sat there like an overgrown schoolgirl, biting my fingers and snorting with barely supressed mirth.

"Are you on drugs?" Paul asked, shocking me so much that I burst out laughing again.

"No," I managed to say.

"Have you been drinking?"

I shook my head and realized that I was getting hysterical. I was literally shaking and nothing was coming out of my mouth except these choked gasps.

"Then I'm at a complete loss as to why you're behaving like a stupid schoolgirl," Paul shouted, his face flushed with rage.

That shocked me into complete silence.

"You are the band. You are the most important person in that bloody group," Paul continued, pointing his finger at me. "And your emotions are getting in the way."

"Sorry," I mumbled. "It's just that my emotions are why I'm in the group, 'cause of the songs and stuff."

Paul rolled his eyes. "The group is not about making great art, it's about making money. The record company doesn't put out your CDs for the benefit of—what do you call it? Girlkind? They do it to make a profit. And the sooner you realize that, the better."

"But, but you said . . . It's not about business, it's about touching people."

"Touching people enough that they part with fifteen quid to buy your album," Paul snapped. "Grow up, Molly. And when I say grow up, I mean start thinking about maturing your songs even if your mind hasn't caught up yet, or I'll get a songwriter in to do it for you."

That moment there. That one moment when Paul spoke those words, his voice oozing contempt, was the end. It was the end of a lot of things. Some of them would actually finish a few months down the line, but right then was the end of a lot of it—including me acting like a silly wide-eyed kid.

Very slowly I got up, walked over to the sink, and started soaking a hand towel in cold water. "I hate you," I said simply. "I violently dislike you. I don't trust you and I don't believe you have my best intentions at heart."

He looked surprised for a second but recovered quickly. "Don't talk about things you don't understand," he said patronizingly. "And we both know why you hate me, don't we?" He looked at me knowingly.

"This is not about the kiss," I said, running the damp cloth over my face. "Though I wish to God it had never happened. I've just realized that actually I'm the one with the power here."

"Is that so?" Paul leaned on the edge of the sink and folded his arms. "I can't wait to hear this."

I lifted my chin and went into battle. "You're right. I *am* the group. It's my group and without me you wouldn't have a job. All the 'don't do this' and 'don't do that' is because you don't want me to realize that I'm the one in control. You're nothing without me."

Paul reached out a hand and gripped my wrist hard enough to hurt. "No, Molly, *you're* nothing without me. You'd still be working in that stupid corner shop and coming home before your curfew if it wasn't for me. I made you, and yeah, I know it's a cliché, but I can break you."

I wasn't buying it. I might be naive and make appalling errors of judgment, but I wasn't stupid. "You can't touch me," I snarled, yanking my hand away. "The album's come out, we're just about to tour America, and if I go to Big Black and say I want you sacked, they'll do it."

Paul was good. Really good. Didn't so much as twitch an eyelash at my threat. "I've got a contract in my office, signed by you, that says otherwise."

"I'll write the songs that I want to write, kiss who I want to kiss, and if I want to look for a new manager, then I'll do that too," I said, as if he hadn't spoken.

"Don't start messing with me, Moll," Paul advised, but there was a nervous tic banging away in his cheek. " 'Cause I fight dirty. Very, very dirty."

Paul and I snarled at each other for a bit longer. Threatening me with all manner of legal (and other) nasties didn't seem to do a whole lot to improve his temper. I knew he was itching to come out with something cliché-ridden like, "I'll see you in court, you little bitch!" but he contented himself with one last vengeful glare in my direction before storming out and slamming the door with enough force that the hinges rattled.

I waited just long enough to make sure that Paul wasn't in my immediate vicinity, and then snatched up my jacket and headed back into the club to find Dean and tell him that we were OK. We were coming out right then, right now. No more secrets. No more lies. No more sneaking around behind everyone's back and getting a crick in my neck from kissing with my head half turned to check that no one was coming. If the Paul-shaped obstacle was out of the way then Dean would stop acting like Mr. Multiple Personality Disorder and become a devoted boyfriend who'd write me poetry, take me to arty French film double bills, and hold my hand when we were walking down the street. He would. He would . . .

He wouldn't because he was standing by the cigarette machine with a lazy smile on his face as Sandrine ran her fingers through his hair, in a way that I knew only too well how much he liked.

I could feel all the blood draining from my face, and I stood there rooted to the spot, unable to move as people jostled around me. I shut my eyes and when I opened them again, Dean and the Hobiscuit were kissing like they hadn't had a decent meal in forever and had decided to devour each other instead.

Eyes full of tears, I stumbled out of the nearest door and found myself on the fire escape. It was strange, I looked up and the stars were so pretty. Some of them didn't even exist anymore, but they were still up there in the sky, twinkling away. I don't know why I always get sidetracked by these random thoughts when my whole world has turned to roadkill. I sat down on the steps and looked at the stars and cried. I cried because Dean had been lying to me and Paul had been lying to me and because I'd been lying to myself. I was just like one of the stars up above me—being forced to shine and glitter even though the real me had ceased to exist a long time ago.

I was wiping my eyes with the sleeve of my jacket when Tara sat down beside me. "Oh, Molly, why are you crying?" she asked, leaning against me and trying to peer at my face.

"Just stuff," I said between sobs. I was this close to telling her about Dean and Paul and the whole messy story, when she put her head on my shoulder and offered me the bottle that she'd been holding.

"Now I know why Jane drinks so much," she giggled. "Makes you forget all the icky things."

The way we were going, Paul wouldn't have to worry about

my emotions splitting up the band, we'd all be in rehab long before that could happen.

"Are you drunk?" I hiccuped. "You shouldn't drink if you're sad—just makes everything worse. Plus, hangovers are never fun. And I speak from experience."

"Aw, Molly, you're so sweet," Tara singsonged, snuggling against me. "I love you."

I patted her knee absently. "Yeah, I love you too."

"No, you don't understand!" she said fiercely. "I *really* love you. Really, really love you."

"I know you do," I sighed. "And you're really, really drunk."

"I'm not that drunk," Tara protested, but she was, 'cause she suddenly pressed her lips against mine.

It was a messy, wet kiss that was completely different from kissing a boy. It was softer, sweeter—and so not the answer.

"Hey, Tara, honey, no," I said gently, leaning back and holding her off with my hands when she tried to kiss me again. "I love you and I'm flattered, but this is wrong. A whole load of wrong."

"No, it's not," she protested. "Not wrong, it's right. I love you!"

I was just about to burst into tears again, because it seemed like a pretty good reaction, when T stepped onto the fire escape. "Jane's really out of it," he muttered, dreads swinging agitatedly. "I think she needs to go home."

That seemed to sober Tara up sharpish. "I want to get out of here too," she snapped, stumbling to her feet and pushing T back through the door.

With a deep sigh, I stood up, brushed down my skirt, and followed them back to the bar, where Jane was slumped on the floor with a crowd of interested bystanders surrounding her.

I pushed my way through the crowd and knelt down at her side. I wasn't quite sure what to do with someone who'd drunk herself into a stupor. I gingerly put my hand on her forehead, but my palm was so hot and sticky, anyway, I couldn't tell if it was her or me who was running a temperature. "Jane, are you OK?" I asked, shaking her very gently. She opened her eyes, raised her head slightly, and then threw up all over me.

It took three of us and a security guard to get Jane into a cab—that's after finding a cab that would actually stop for us. Jane stayed more or less out of it, only stirring every now and again to mumble incoherently and make retching noises. Just as the taxi was pulling up outside their flat and T was paying the driver, she leaned forward and puked again. I threw some tissues on the little pool of vomit and dragged her out before the driver noticed.

Getting her upstairs involved me tugging her hands while T and Tara shoved her from behind. Then she decided that all she really wanted to do was lie on the hall carpet and kick her legs about so we could all see her red knickers.

I couldn't help but wonder if I was this annoying when I got drunk. Then I remembered that the three times I'd been inebriated had ended up in me a) snogging Dean, b) snogging Paul, and c) losing my virginity—so I really wasn't in a position to chastise Jane for showing off her underwear.

"Jane, I really think you'd be better off in bed," Tara said helplessly, ten minutes later as we still crouched in the hall, while I ineffectually dabbed at Jane's face with a flannel.

"Go 'way," was all the response we got.

We gave up trying to talk some sense into Jane and retreated into the bathroom. "I think she needs to go to hospital," I announced. "Maybe she's got alcohol poisoning. I've never seen her like this. I mean, I know she drinks a lot but . . . What?"

T had gone milky white. "Don't think she's just been drinking," he said unhappily. "I think she's taken some stuff."

I looked at him blankly for a second before a little lightbulb clicked on above my head. "Oh. OH! Oh, oh you mean . . ."

He nodded. "There was this shifty guy hanging about all afternoon, and I saw him in the Gents, and he was, erm, y'know, doing deals."

I fixed him with a look. "No! No way would Jane do drugs. I *know* her and she just wouldn't. She's my best friend, and we tell each other everything!"

T shrugged and muttered something under his breath.

"Huh?"

"He said that Jane does a lot of things that you don't know about—like drinking lager with her breakfast, sleeping with a different guy every night, and doing these." Tara held out her hand and showed me the little white tablets resting on her palm.

I sat down heavily on the edge of the bath. "Everything's falling apart," I whispered.

"Maybe we should ring Paul . . ." I heard Tara say.

"No. Not Paul," I said firmly. "Look, help me get Jane into bed and we'll make her drink loads of water, and I'll sit with her and make sure that she's . . . she . . ."

"Doesn't choke on her own vomit?" Tara suggested in a pissed-off voice that was completely out of character. "You think you're so intuitive, Molly, but you don't *see* anything." And she turned and walked out of the bathroom.

Reprinted by kind permission of *Foxy* magazine

The Rumour Mill

It was rock 'n' roll Babylon at the launch party for The Hormones' debut album last Valentine's Day. Confirming those 'are they?/aren't they?' rumours was singer Molly, who seems to be no longer reluctant or a virgin, given the way that she yanked guitarist Dean in for a long, slow smooch with tongues in front of a gaggle of photographers. The band's management were quick to scotch stories of romance blossoming on tour, and a spokesman for the band insisted that 'Molly was just playing up for the cameras.'

The spin machine had to really crank up, though, when bassist Jane, living up to her reputation as the female Liam Gallagher, collapsed in the bar. The official line was 'nervous exhaustion' but that didn't stop her from vomiting on the hapless Molly.

With such dissent in the ranks, it's no wonder that the band are meeting for crisis talks on the eve of their first American tour, supporting the equally hard-living Sons of Lee Marvin.

The day before we were due to fly to the States, Paul called an emergency band meeting. He said it was "to clear the air," but I got the feeling that we were all out of industrial strength Glade PlugIns. Tara wasn't talking to me after the fire-escape fiasco and the tense bathroom scene. And when Jane had woken up the next morning (thankfully I'd not had to clear her airways of obstructions during the night), she'd flatly denied taking any strange substances or even drinking too much. "I just ate a dodgy prawn sandwich," she'd snapped and refused to discuss it any further.

Dean had been maintaining radio silence, and T, now that he'd started talking, made everyone wish that he hadn't. Everything that came out of his mouth was a dour observation about life and our own pathetic methods of dealing with it.

So The Hormones who sat in Paul's office were not happy bunnies. Independently of one another, we'd all decided to wear black—and any passerby would have mistaken us for a funeral party who'd got lost on the way home, as we slumped in varied poses of somber colored dejection.

Paul waited until we were all clutching coffees and cleared his throat. "There's a lot of tension between you all, and we have a crucial couple of months coming up," he began, playing nervously with the "Greetings from Las Vegas" snow globe on his desk. "I want this session to be an opportunity for you all to say what's pissing you off. But it's not about blame or finger-pointing. Stick to 'I feel' statements: 'I feel confused.' 'I feel overwhelmed.' Now who wants to begin?"

Everybody's hand shot up but mine.

"Jane?"

"OK, I feel hurt at the way everybody's been treating me like a complete alky. I had food poisoning."

Tara snorted. "I feel really annoyed with Jane for lying when I know that she drinks all the time."

"Right, well, I feel angry that nobody trusts me to tell the truth. Do you want me to do a pee test every time we go on stage so you can check my alcohol levels?" Jane grumbled.

I could see that Paul was grinding down on his expensively capped back molars. "I don't think that will be necessary, Jane. Let's just say that Tara's raised her concerns about you and you'll do what you can to ease them. Agreed?"

Jane and Tara nodded and glared at the same time, like two evil monkeys.

"Dean, do you want to go next?"

Dean sat up and glanced at me, but I turned my head away and looked at the Rothko print that Paul had on the wall.

"I feel unappreciated," Dean stated. "Molly gets all the attention and people think that we're her backing band. I want full acknowledgment of my contributions to the band and I know that Jane does too. We write the songs with—"

"You *help* write the songs," I chimed in, but Paul held up his hand.

"Stick with the 'I feel' statements, please."

"I feel a deeply held conviction that I write the bulk of the songs," I bit out. "The only assistance I get from Jane is the odd word, and Dean does some of the chord work on the choruses. And I also feel very tired of getting the blame for being the front woman when our manager has constantly overridden my express wish that other members of the band get to do press too."

This was Jane and Dean's cue to shoot filthy looks at Paul, who pretended that he hadn't seen them and contented himself with the comment, "You're not really understanding the structure of the 'I feel' statements, Molly."

"I *feel* that you're patronizing me, *Paul*," I snapped back.

"This is about you guys," Paul said, in a reasonable voice that was completely at odds with the flash of anger in his eyes. "We can talk about any higher-level problems at a later date."

"I feel like this is a waste of time," T suddenly announced. "We all know what the real issue is, but no one has the guts to say anything."

"I feel happy that T is bringing this up," Jane agreed.

"I feel happier," Tara added.

I knew what was coming—I didn't know *how* they knew. I just knew that they knew, though Dean was investigating his muffin like he had no idea that we were about to be—

"Dean and Molly had been boinking each other's brains out and then having disruptive, upsetting arguments to put us off the scent. And that's what the real problem is," Jane snarled. "And do I need to mention that you've both lied to us and created a crappy atmosphere to work in?"

At that point there should have been a stunned silence, but the only person who looked shell-shocked was Paul, who'd obviously thought we hadn't progressed beyond a little light petting.

I put my hands over my face and couldn't look at anyone, but I heard Dean chuckle slightly and say under his breath, "Well, that's that, then." He seemed to be taking it very well.

"Do either of you want to apologize for the way you've let down your friends?" Paul asked in a strangulated voice.

I rested my head on my knees and tried to concentrate on taking deep, even breaths.

"Oh, for God's sake, stop being such a drama queen," Jane said in a bored voice. "So they've been shagging. It's not like they tried to assassinate the queen. It would have been nice if my oldest friend had decided to let me know, though."

"Yeah, it's not the sex, it's the covering up of the sex," Tara pointed out. "If we'd known you were in a relationship then maybe we'd have acted differently."

"I'm sorry," I whispered, taking my hands away from my face long enough to send Tara a glance that tried to convey my sincerity and my regret and all points in between. "It's just that Paul said that interband relationships—"

"We don't need to go into convoluted explanations," Paul interjected hastily. "Has anyone got any more earth-shattering revelations? . . . No. I think when the American tour is out of the way, you need to take some time away from one another. But this has helped."

"It couldn't have made things any worse," Jane hissed at Tara as we left Paul's office.

Which just went to show how little she knew.

I was going to shuffle off to Pauline's and do some pop-starry stuff like putting my washing in the tumble dryer and packing. The others were talking about getting some food to take back to the flat. And if they rented a DVD would they have time to return it on the way to the airport? And did they really want to watch *Austin Powers* again? I didn't feel like I was in their gang. Don't ask me why. It might have been the way they were all acting like everything was going to be OK, whereas I had this impending sense of doom, like I was about to go into hospital for open-heart surgery.

"I'm gonna head back to Finchley then," I said, giving them a halfhearted wave. "So I'll see you at the airport tomorrow?"

"Aren't you coming back with us?" Jane asked. "I even promise not to make sarcastic comments when you and Dean actually realize you're allowed to snuggle on the sofa."

I pulled a face. "Firstly, ewwww, and secondly, no. I have stuff to do."

"So the idea of snuggling with me repulses you? Cheers, Moll," Dean teased.

What could I say? It wasn't the time to start a slanging match about his tongue-heavy reunion with the Hobiscuit. For one second, I had this strange urge to jump in a cab, go to King's Cross, and take the first train back to Southport, so I could climb into my bed and stay there until I was older and less stupid—or at least until Mum stopped making me medicinal bowls of vegetarian chicken soup and told me to snap out of it. In the end, I settled for a lopsided smile and some excuse about "that time of the month" and we went our separate ways.

But when I got back to Pauline's, she took one look at my face and held out her arms. And I let her cuddle me and stroke my hair while refusing to tell her what the matter was.

"Do you want to phone your mum?" she asked worriedly, after half an hour of me lying with my head on her lap and not speaking.

I pulled a "no power on this earth will make me phone home" face.

Pauline sighed. "You know, Molly, for someone who claims to be doing exactly what she wants, you don't seem very happy."

"I'm fine," I mumbled. "It's just this tour . . ."

"Do you want me to ring your manager and say you're not well? Maybe they could cancel it?"

And that was it, really. This wasn't a French test that I could get out of with a letter from my mum saying that I was sick. It was full-on, big-time responsibility with thousands and thousands of pounds at stake if I didn't get on that plane.

"I'm OK," I mumbled. "I'm just being silly. Shall we watch *EastEnders*?"

I was lying in bed later on, staring at the ceiling, when the *Itchy and Scratchy* ring tone on my phone kicked in. It was dark, so I didn't look to see who was calling. But it was after midnight and calls that late were usually bad news. Maybe the others had been struck by a meteor on the way back from the video shop and Paul had agreed to postpone the tour until we could find replacements.

"Hello?"

"Moll, it's me."

"Oh. It's really late, Dean. I was asleep."

"Yeah, sorry about that. You just seemed sad today and I wanted to speak to you before I went to bed."

"I saw you that night."

"Which night?"

"I saw you with Sandrine. You pushed me away and Paul bawled us out, and when I went back into the club, you and Sandrine were snogging each other's faces off. I saw you."

"And you jumped to the conclusion that I'm a complete bastard who was just using you while she was away."

"What other conclusion should I have jumped to?"

"What about the one where I see my ex-girlfriend and I kiss her good-bye . . ."

"And the excess saliva is just your way of letting you know you'll miss her?"

"God, Molly, there were no tongues, because I'm involved with this other girl! Though I don't know why, because most of the time this other girl's a pain in the arse."

"Yeah, well, I know that girl and she's actually nice and funny—and confused because the boy that she really likes is mean to her and only acknowledges their coupledom when their friends out them. And she has fantastic dress sense."

"I know that boy. He's an idiot. Doesn't know how lucky he is to have that girl, and he's secretly pleased that everybody knows they're dating so he can indulge in disgusting and inappropriate public displays of affection with her."

"Oh . . . well, maybe I should tell the girl that."

"Yeah, maybe you should. So, you still sulking?"

"Haven't decided."

"You know you're completely irrational, don't you?"

"I am not! . . . I *do* want the band to be a partnership, Dean. You have to believe that. I want you and Jane and Tara and God—even T, if he stopped sounding so doom and gloom—to do press. But the songs are mine. They're all that I have. They're the only thing that makes me special."

"They're not the only thing that makes you special, Molly. There are lots of things that make you special. But, look we'll sort it out. We'll sort everything out."

"I wish we weren't doing this tour. I actually missed my parents today for, like, the first time ever."

"It'll be fine. We'll have a great time. Hey, we're going to America and I'm glad that I'm going with you."

"Now you're just laying it on too thick!"

"You think? I thought I sounded all sexy and devoted."

"I'm glad you phoned. It means a lot that you called and we sorted things out. I just wish life wasn't so complicated. Would you still want to go out with me if we were back in Southport and I was working in Best Buys?"

"Yeah, you looked cute in that overall. I have a fetish for man-made fibers."

"OK, I'm hanging up now."

"Wait! What are you wearing? Those pajamas with the rabbits on them? Or the ones with the dots—'cause you look hot in them too."

"I'm hanging up."

"I'll see you tomorrow then, Moll."

"Yeah, see you tomorrow."

"I wish you were here now. Don't s'pose you fancy having phone sex?"

"Dean! Good night."

"Yeah, good night, Moll. Love you."

"Oh, oh, um, I lo—"

Click.

Pause.

"Dean, you still there?"

Pause.

Click.

Reprinted by kind permission of *Excess* magazine, USA. Excerpt from "New York Music Seminar Report"

UNDERAGE AND OVER HERE

Kicking off the opening night of the New York Music Seminar were Brit hopefuls The Hormones. Although not one of them is old enough to drink in this country, what they lack in experience, they make up for in youthful exuberance.

They play a weird hybrid of cartoon pop mixed with a punk aesthetic, and lead singer, Molly Montgomery, oozes star quality with every wiggle of her skinny hips. From the poignancy of the UK hit "I Can See My Life From Here" to the giddy-round-the-gills geekiness of "Magic Marker Love" and "Hello Kitty Speedboat," The Hormones are definitely one to watch.

This is the kind of band that starts revolutions.

It all began so well.

Our first American date was at a music conference in New

York and tickets for our show were being scalped by the touts outside for one hundred dollars. We were the hottest act in town and everyone wanted to hang out with us.

After our set (where the crowd refused to budge until we played our first ever encore), we went to this famous club called CBGB and I met Jo X who used to play guitar with Ruby. Paul, no matter how pissed off he was with me, couldn't resist introducing us, knowing full well that he'd earn mucho brownie points. "This is Molly—please be nice to her or I'll never hear the end of it," Paul had said when we'd bumped into Jo outside the cloakroom. And before I could thump Paul or at least glare at him, Jo had kissed my hand and asked if I wanted to hang.

We all squashed into a booth in the back room while Dean badgered Jo about all the myths around him and Ruby: "Is it true that you once smashed all your instruments on stage?" and "Did you really spit in Kurt Cobain's face and accuse him of ripping off one of your tunes for the chorus of 'Smells Like Teen Spirit'?" and "Did Ruby really chase Courtney Love down the street threatening to beat her to death with her guitar?"

Jo X kept laughing, but when Dean suddenly lost interest and began kissing the side of my neck while I squirmed deliciously, his battered, broken face suddenly looked even more battered and broken. When Dean slipped out of the booth to see if he could persuade Paul to buy us some booze, Jo X turned to me. "You remind me a lot of Ruby," he murmured. "How she was, anyway."

"Do I?" I squeaked excitedly.

"But the difference is that Ruby started believing her own

publicity, and I hope that you're too smart to do that," he commented darkly.

He peered at me intently. I noticed that his pale hands were shaking, and I wondered if the rumors about his smack habit were true.

"Whatever happened to Ruby?" I asked to distract him from staring at me. "She hasn't released anything in ages."

Jo took a long sip from his bottle of beer. "Oh, kid," he said, his lips twisting. "Don't ask questions that you really don't want to know the answers to."

There was an awkward pause while I tried to figure out what the deal was with the cryptic.

"It's just, Ruby's my heroine," I ventured. "She was my inspiration for starting a band. She's like this cool rebel queen who has this—I don't know—this unshakeable belief in herself. She gives me something to aspire to."

Jo leaned in closer to me. I could see the scar on his eyebrow, the result of a notorious fight between him and Joey Ramone. "Just remember that the only person you can trust is yourself. Trust no one. Not your smooth-talking manager or that pretty boy who can't keep his hands off you. 'Cause in this business everyone wants a piece of you and you end up with nothing. Nothing." He banged his bottle down hard on the tabletop and I jumped. "Hey, kid," he cajoled. "I didn't mean to scare ya. I'm just old and bitter."

Then Dean came back and started asking Jo about whether he was still doing music, and I dismissed his twisted words. But it left me with an unsettled feeling like I was moving underwater, and everything was slow and labored, when before it had been so fast that it was all I could do to keep up.

Life continued to be happy-shaped when Paul flew back to England the next day, with promises to meet up with us for the last date of the tour in L.A. I was glad to see the back of his be-suited smarminess. But it was like Paul had taken the good luck with him, because we started fighting again the minute we stepped onto our dilapidated tour bus—which Dean immediately christened Disgracelands.

In the end, it wasn't me and Dean's secret sex or Jane's access all areas excess or even Tara *still* being mad with me over those five minutes on the fire escape that tore us apart. In truth, breaking America broke our spirits.

Our time was measured out in hours spent in crappy clubs and concert halls with tiny dressing rooms that smelled of stale beer and vomit. On the walls would be names and dates and dirty pictures scrawled by the ghostly fingers of hundreds of other bands who'd made the same pilgrimage as us. And there were the hours cooped up in Disgracelands, driving down these endless interstates, that were only broken up by strip malls and drive-through McDonald's.

We were playing forty-two dates in fifty days, and the pace of getting from A (for Anchorage) to B (for Boston) didn't allow for overnight stops. It was all right for the Sons of Lee Marvin, they were a big MTV band who could afford to fly themselves (and their huge entourage of roadies and hard-faced "girlfriends") to each different town on the schedule. But when we rolled into the venue's parking lot, whitefaced through lack of sleep and decent nutritionally balanced meals, we'd usually find that their tour manager had decided that there wasn't time to let us sound check. And because they wouldn't let us use their gear (most groups are cool enough to allow you to share their amps and sound equipment), we'd barely have enough time to set up. Most nights, we'd sneak on stage to loud boos from the crowd who were only there to see the headline act, and we'd have to spend the first few minutes of our set crouching down to tune our instruments. Not surprisingly, we mostly sucked.

We tried to take it on the chin. All of us but Dean, who on the fifth night of no sound check burst into the Sons of Lee Marvin's well-appointed dressing room and tried to reason it out with them.

The first I knew about it was when Frank, our tour manager, came running up to me as I helped Tim, our roadie, pack up my gear. "You need to talk to Dean," Frank puffed. "He's going to get himself into trouble."

"He'll be fine," I dismissed airily. "He's just going to talk to them, y'know, musician to musician. They were a support band once."

"Yeah and now they're a bunch of arrogant gits who don't want you stealing their glory," Frank pointed out. "And Dean is not famed for his diplomacy."

I rolled my eyes, before meeting Frank's worried gaze. "Oh, God, he's going to open his mouth and make everything so much worse," I sighed. "C'mon, we'll drag him out of the lion's den."

But it was too late for that. As we hurried down the corridor to their dressing room, the door opened—to be followed by an airborne Dean, who landed in a heap on the floor.

"Get your skinny punk ass out of here," I heard someone shout.

Frank and I started running toward Dean, who struggled to his knees.

"What is your damage?" Dean spluttered, and then to my horror, I saw him spit a mouthful of blood on the ground.

"You're only on this tour because your record company bought your support slot," their big bruiser of a tour manager informed Dean, coming to stand in the doorway. "No refunds, so deal with it."

"Dean! You're bleeding!" I cried, squatting down to look at his face, which was already purpling with the promise of bruises.

"If you want to sound check, maybe you should get your girl-friend to come in here and ask real nice," leered a voice from the open door, and there was a collective cackle and the clink of bottles.

Dean lunged forward, and Frank and I held him back while the door slammed shut.

"It's not worth it," Frank advised him, pulling Dean upright. "Look, nobody breaks America on their first go. At least you're getting your faces known."

"And your face has looked better," I told Dean ruefully, stroking a gentle finger along his brow. "You're going to have a black eye."

"Wankers!" Dean snarled, and flinched away from me. Then he limped off down the corridor.

I went to follow him, but Frank put a warning hand on my arm. "Let him go and lick his wounds for a bit," he said. "He probably feels a bit stupid and doesn't want you fussing over him."

I was hurt, but I was fast learning that tour managers are like Yoda and have great wisdom in all matters, so I let Dean go.

The next crisis hit a few days later, when we actually had the luxury of staying in a Best Western motel on an overnight stop in Dayton, Ohio. It was such a relief to get off the bus that we ended up having a wild party in mine and Dean's room with some kids who'd come to see us at the end of the show and told us "You rock, man!"

Dean and I had already had words that day when I'd insisted on hauling the contents of our suitcases to the nearest Laundromat instead of "having a lie-down." Our clothes were *ripe*, but more than that, I just needed to have some time to myself. I hadn't even been able to pee in peace without somebody banging on the bus's bathroom door and telling me to hurry up.

Dean was also pissed off because I wouldn't share a bunk with him. I'd slept with him one night on the bus and it was an experience that I didn't want to repeat. Ever. The bunk was narrow, and me and Dean were narrow, which was a recipe for elbows in ribs and sharp pointy angles. And although there was no way we were going to do "that," every time one of us even tugged at the blanket, Jane and Tara and even T—God rot him—would yell out: "Will you two get a room!" Oh, excuse me while I split my sides laughing.

So, anyway, this party. Our new friends went on a beer run and came back with a couple of kegs, and hooked up their car stereo to one of our amps, and we were all chililng out and grooving. Dean's arm rested loosely around my waist, and every now and then he'd plant a kiss on my cheek or whisper some sweet bit of nothingness in my ear. I was generally feeling at one with the world.

Out of the corner of my eye, I saw Jane disappear into the bathroom with one of the American guys who swore blind that his name was Chip and couldn't understand why we found this hysterically funny. I decided that Jane was old enough to take care of herself—it wasn't like she was drinking that much, anyway.

Dean and I were sitting outside on the steps, smooching under the stars and listening to the throaty chirping of the cicadas, when we heard a commotion coming rom the room.

"What's all the noise?" I asked crossly, coming up for air.

Dean leaned in to capture my lips again and I got lost in the moment—until we heard a loud crash, followed by a couple of thumps.

"We'll get kicked out if they don't calm down," Dean tutted, gently disentangling himself from my arms and standing up.

I pouted a bit, but when Dean stuck out his hand, I took it and let him pull me up.

"We should kick them all out," I said decisively. "So we can party all by ourselves."

"I like the sound of that," Dean drawled as I followed him into the room with my hand in the back pocket of his trousers—only to be confronted by the sight of Jane, in jeans and a bra, balanced precariously on top of the table.

"Who wants a lap dance?" she was shrieking, her face flushed and her eyes like black holes, while Tara tried to coax her down.

The American boys looked shocked. I mean, this was a small town, and I think the only excitement they got was at the local school's big football games. They certainly didn't seem to be used to the sight of drunken English girls trying to take their clothes off.

Dean marched over to the stereo and turned it off. "Jane, you're going to break your neck," he shouted. "Get down!"

"You're not my boss!" Jane said, wagging her finger. "Now shall I take my bra or my jeans off?"

"How much have you had to drink? You promised me you'd only have two beers!" Tara exclaimed, almost in tears. "I hate you when you're drunk."

"I don't care!"

I turned to the American boys. "Maybe you should go," I suggested. "It's been a really long day and I think we're all a bit tired."

They didn't need to be told twice. They were all like, "Hey, man, it was great hanging but, like, y'know, I have to be home before my curfew," and other things that I thought people only said in bad teen movies. Within five minutes, they'd cleared out, taking the unfinished keg and the stereo with them.

Jane was still wobbling and refusing all pleas to move to a more stable surface. "You're no fun," she spat as she attempted an uncoordinated bump and grind, which made the table lurch alarmingly. "You're all boring."

She carried on like this for a bit longer, with Dean shouting and Tara crying, until T simply walked over, grabbed her by the knees, and lifted her down in a fireman's carry—with her thumping on his back.

T carried Jane over to the bed, and as she tried to dislodge his grip, a little bag full of pills slipped out of her back pocket. No one seemed to notice, and while T and Tara were holding Jane down, I quickly picked them up and stuffed them into the bedside drawer. As I straightened up, I saw Dean looking at me with a confused expression on his face—which swiftly turned to realization. I looked away. Now wasn't the time.

Meanwhile, Tara had got a bottle of water from the minibar and before anyone could stop her, had upended it all over Jane's flailing body.

Jane sat up with a jolt. "Jesus! What did you do that for?" she gasped indignantly, sounding furious but more like herself. "Oh, God, I'm going to bed. And stop looking at my tits." She flounced out of the room like a platinum-tipped whirlwind, with Tara trailing after her unhappily.

"Well, she got her money's worth out of *two* glasses of beer," T remarked dourly, gathering up his jacket. "See you in the morning. Sorry about your bed."

Dean and I were left standing amid the debris of the party. I started picking up the empty Cheetos bags and cigarette packets, while Dean stripped the covers on the bed.

"You OK?" I asked, but he just shrugged.

We remade the bed in silence, and then I went into the bathroom to take off my makeup and clean my teeth and prepare myself for the big showdown that I knew was coming. And when I reemerged I wasn't the least bit surprised to see Dean sitting on the bed, holding the bag of pills.

"Did you know about this?" he said accusingly before I'd even stepped into the room.

I stalled for time by picking up my brush and running it through my hair.

"I said, did you know about this?" Dean bit out.

"Kind of," I sighed. "That night we did a showcase, T thought Jane might have taken something. But we weren't sure."

Dean spilled the tablets out on the bed and ran a finger through them. "What are they? Ecstasy? Uppers? Junior Dispirin?"

I sat down next to him and looked at the pills spread out accusingly between us. They looked so innocuous. "I don't know," I admitted. "They could be anything. They could be antihistamines!"

Dean raised his eyebrows skeptically and snorted.

"Dean, I don't think we should jump to conclusions. She probably just had too much to drink. You know how she gets."

"Yeah, I know how she gets when she's drunk," he said scathingly. "And it's not like this."

I touched his arm. "Look, we'll talk to her in the morning. *I'll* talk to her. We should get some sleep.

He looked like he was going to disagree, but then his shoulders slumped. "Whatever."

It took me ages to get to sleep. Despite the fact that we had our own room and a double bed all to ourselves, Dean and I lay there without touching. At one stage, I curled up against him and reached out to tousle his hair, but he murmured a protest and moved away.

When I woke up (so I guess I *had* managed to sleep), Dean wasn't in bed. I sat up and saw him standing over me. He looked cold and distant, even though the benign face of Afro Ken on his T-shirt beamed at me.

"What time is it?" I groaned. "You should have woken me."

"I want her out of the band," Dean stated baldly. "If she's doing drugs, she's out. I've . . . *We've* worked too hard to let her screw things up because she wants to become some tired, old, rock 'n' roll cliché."

"I said I'll talk to her," I snapped.

"Fine. Do it," Dean ordered, and turned and walked out.

After a blistering hot shower that soothed all my bus-induced aches but only 10 percent of my inner angst, I wandered over to Tara and Jane's room and knocked on the door.

Tara looked relieved but exhausted when she saw me standing there.

"I brought breakfast," I announced too brightly, holding up the bag of doughnuts that I'd bought from the Krispy Kreme across the road.

"She's still in bed," Tara hissed in my ear. "Spent half the night throwing up. I've had no sleep."

I could just make out the top of Jane's head. The rest of her was burrowed under the bedclothes. "Hey you," I said softly, sitting down next to her motionless form. I tentatively prodded her, and she moaned and turned over. "I got doughnuts," I added. "They're all fresh and warm and yummy."

"Not hungry," came the muffled reply.

Tara left the room, slamming the door behind her. I took that as my cue to pull the covers off Jane. I was through with being nice and understanding.

"Listen to me, Jane. I've got your bag of fun in my pocket," I began, not bothering to hide my annoyance. "Want to explain exactly what they are?"

Jane shuffled around a bit and tried to bury her face in the pillow, until I grabbed it from her.

"Pills," I growled. "What have you been taking? And why the hell were you mixing them with alcohol? Did those afternoons in health class mean nothing to you?"

That hit home. She opened bloodshot eyes and glared at me. "I don't know what you're talking about."

"OK, so you won't mind if I go and flush them down the loo then, will you?" I announced, and stood up to move bathroomward.

Jane scrambled across the bed. "Give them back! They're mine!" She reached around me to grab the bag, but I managed to hold her back.

"What are they?" I shouted. "What are you doing to yourself?"

"They're just hay-fever tablets," she said sullenly.

It hurt that she could lie so lamely to *me*. That she didn't know me any better than that, after all that we'd been through. And that I didn't know her anymore. She was my best friend and I was at a complete loss to understand anything she did anymore.

"Look, Dean's going mad," I said, trying another tack. "He wants you out of the band if you're doing drugs. But I think I've managed to—"

"It's got nothing to do with him," Jane sneered, moving toward her open suitcase and rummaging through it for her wash bag. "I might have known you'd take his side."

"This is not about taking sides," I protested. "It's about someone I love being all self-destructive and then lying to me about it."

Jane sneered again. "God! Could you be any more of a drama queen?" She walked toward the bathroom but before she could close the door, I wedged myself in the gap.

"Jane! Please! I'm trying to help but I don't know how," I pleaded, hoping that somehow I could touch her. "C'mon, this is me. If you're unhappy, if you're feeling lost, you have me. You will always have me."

Jane smiled in this hollow, empty way that didn't reach her eyes. "You don't get it, Molly, do you?"

"I might, if you explained it to me," I said. I moved toward her, but she stepped back.

"Nothing to explain," she insisted. "They're just hay-fever pills—and note to self: Don't mix them with beer. Now can I have a shower or are you going to stay and make sure I don't try and inhale my shampoo?"

Cut to two weeks later and we're eating breakfast in a diner on Interstate 101 just by the Golden Gate Bridge in San Francisco. It was our on-tour daily routine. Frank and Tim were discussing how long it would take to get to the venue. T was scraping Tara's mushrooms onto his plate. Jane was drinking her third cup of black coffee. Dean's knees were bumping against mine under the table, even though he was still angry with me for refusing to listen to his threats and insinuations about Jane.

I picked up the bottle of Heinz tomato ketchup and was just about to shake out a good-sized dollop to mop up the last of my fries, when I realized it was the exact same bottle that we had on our kitchen table at home. If it was ten in the morning here, it was six o'clock in the evening there. Dad would have just got in from work and be helping Mum to make dinner, while Joss did his homework and drove them mad with his theories on deep space travel. I could hear his chatter: "And wormholes, Mum, do you know why they're called wormholes? It's not because of worms. Mum, you're not listening to me!"

My hands started shaking so hard that I dropped the bottle. It landed on the floor with a crash that made everyone jump, but I was pushing my plate away so I could slump over the table and put my head in my hands and cry. I don't know how long they sat there watching me sob. It was like I wasn't there. There was jut a girl with her hands over her face, weeping.

When I came back from wherever I'd been, I was lying down on one of the bunks while Frank sat cross-legged next to me and made soothing noises as he patted my shoulder.

He didn't start bombarding me with questions, for which I was eternally grateful, just let me sit up and handed me a tissue. I felt absolutely numb. Like there was nothing left inside me.

All of a sudden the curtain parted, and Tara poked her head through. "Are you all right?" she asked in a worried little voice.

I nodded blankly.

"Just tour blues," said Frank safely. "Happens to everyone. I think Molly needs a bit of peace and quiet. Let her get some rest."

I was happy just to lie there, slightly worried that my brain seemed to have taken a vacation but, y'know, not *that* worried.

Jane climbed up at one stage with a bottle of water for me, but obviously didn't know what to say, while I sat there with a face like one o'clock half struck. "Just wanted to give you this," she mumbled uncomfortably, shoving the drink at me.

I must have dozed off because next time I opened my eyes, Dean was standing there, arms resting on the edge of the bunk. "Is this about me?" he asked quietly. "Is this because we haven't got on since Jane went mental in Dayton?"

"It's not about you," I murmured, my voice sounding rusty. "I don't know what it's about. I feel very strange."

"What kind of strange?" Dean wanted to know.

I pulled a tired face. "I can't talk about it."

"But you're well enough to go on tonight, aren't you?" he persisted.

"I guess."

"Y'know, Molly, most of the time when I'm with you, I feel like you're not even there," he said angrily, and practically ripped the curtain shut in his haste not to look at me.

I knew what he meant. *I* didn't even know where I was anymore. Oh, geographically, I knew that we were heading toward L.A., but part of me had got lost somewhere in America and I didn't know where to begin looking for it.

So I did what I always did when I didn't know what else to do; I wrote a song about it. A bloody good one too.

Missy and Me
   Words and Music by Molly Montgomery
   Additional music by Dean Speed

Missy lets me see the places where the other boys don't go
She can make me feel like it isn't so
Missy and me ride out into the night
She can take my loneliness and make it alright

Chorus—
   But Missy always lets me down
   Even when she's mine

Missy was the brightest star
Till she lost her shine

Missy and me talk without saying any words
She wants to be as free as the birds
Missy always says she wants to understand
But she holds the truth in her hand

— Chorus —

Missy and me were never built to last
Died too young and lived too fast
Missy is the one thing I can't hold
Takes my heart and leaves it cold

Chorus—
But Missy always lets me down
Even when she's mine
Missy was the brightest star
Till she lost her shine

Missy was the brightest star
till she lost her shine
Missy was the brightest star
till she lost her shine

— Repeat till fade —

• • •

I emerged from my day's weirdness still feeling like a hollow girl. I did the show on autopilot, wearing the old pair of jeans and the Kylie T-shirt that I'd had on all day. I could hear myself singing and playing the guitar, but my face was frozen. I acknowledged the applause (we were making some headway with the Sons of Lee Marvin's following) with a small smile and a nod of my head, but I couldn't get off the stage quick enough.

As I followed the others out into the wings, I saw Paul talking to Frank, the stage lights casting dancing shadows on his face. And I suddenly realized exactly what it was I'd lost—and how to get it back. I knew what I was going to do. Felt it right down in my bones.

Frank bustled the others out of the dressing room before they'd even had a chance to catch their collective breath. "Food, bus, sleep," he told them grimly, leaving me and Paul alone. I stood there, swinging my arms round, while Paul sat on one of our packing cases and crossed his legs. He was wearing a black suit and a black shirt. He looked like a trendy undertaker who'd come to bury me.

I caught a glimpse of my face in the mirror, and I looked pale, older than I had this morning. The Very Cherry hair dye was really doing me no favors.

"So Frank says you hit the wall today," Paul commented, glancing at me curiously. "Happens to everyone. It's been a long tour."

"I'm leaving," I said as if he hadn't spoken. "I quit. After the tour, I'm going home."

Paul sighed. "Is this about me?" he wanted to know.

It made me smile that everyone thought they were to blame, when really it was me.

I shook my head. "It's not you. Not really. I just don't want to do this anymore. Don't want to *be* this."

"You'll feel differently when the tour's finished," Paul argued. "These long-haul American tours are soul destroying."

"I can't do it anymore," I tried to explain. "This isn't what I want. I don't think I ever wanted this. I would have been happy just playing sweet sixteen parties and writing songs for myself."

Paul's patience reached the end of its tether. I was amazed it had lasted as long as it had.

"You don't get to quit because life on the road doesn't live up to your expectations," he snapped. "Take some time off and sort it out."

"Haven't you heard a word I've said?" I hissed, twisting my fingers anxiously. "We all hate each other. We can't bear to share breathing space. I'm losing myself. I don't know who I am anymore."

"Well, you'd better find yourself. Quick," Paul suddenly roared. He jumped up, and in two long strides he had hard hands on my shoulders and was shaking me. "Get. A. Grip."

"I'm quitting," I repeated, making no move to snatch myself away from the hard bite of his hands. "After the tour, I'm leaving."

He let me go. "You're not going anywhere. You signed yourself into an unbreakable contract, and I own your arse for the next ten years."

"I'll get a lawyer to say I was drunk and . . . and . . . and there were witnesses," I blustered, suddenly feeling something. OK, it was icy cold fear—but at least it was something.

"Listen, sweetheart, I can afford bigger, badder lawyers than you," Paul said nastily. "And I'll have you so tied up in legal fees that your great-grandchildren will be struggling to pay them off. Now get on that sodding bus."

"Fine, whatever," I agreed dully. But then that tiny flicker of fury kicked in again. "But this isn't over." And Paul was right in my face, those smooth features contorted by rage into something ugly.

"You keep this between us," he threatened. "You tell the others about this and I'll kill you."

And though I knew he wasn't about to cosh me on the head with an amp and bury my sorry corpse in the Nevada desert, I was freaked out enough to let him have the last word. For now. Plan A might not have worked. I'd just have to come up with a Plan B.

When we got on Disgracelands, Paul shoved me into a seat and then sat down next to me, effectively blocking any escape routes. I don't know what he imagined I was going to do. Jump out of the bus while we were hightailing it down the freeway?

I rested my head against the window, while he slumped next to me, fingers drumming noiselessly against his knees. God, how I hated him.

As the last two dates of the tour were all in L.A., Paul had booked us into a hotel. We checked in early, having driven through the night. Paul promptly disappeared, beckoning Dean and Frank with a terse flick of his hand in the direction of the dining room.

The remaining four of us took the elevator up to our floor in silence. There was nothing left to say to one another.

But as I made my way down the corridor to my room, leaving the others to go in the opposite direction, Jane suddenly ran and caught up with me. "Molly," she breathed urgently. "I . . . God, this sounded much better in my head. Look, I'm sorry about all the stupid stunts I've pulled. And I know you're going through . . . stuff."

"I'm—"

"No, let me finish," she interrupted. "Whatever you decide, I want you to know that I love you and I'll support you. Urgh, I sound like Oprah Winfrey."

Then she was enveloping me in this tight, desperate hug, which just about made me come undone. I breathed in the scent of the rose perfume she wore and let her hair tickle my face.

"How did you know?" I choked out.

Jane held me at arm's length so I could see the resolute expression in her pale green eyes.

"You're still my best friend, Moll. Have been since kindergarten so I know."

I nodded. "I'll see you in a few hours, I really need to crash."

She gave me one final squeeze.

Back in my room I pulled the drapes closed, blocking out the relentless sunlight. I shrugged out of my clothes and collapsed under the covers of the enormous bed. I fell asleep immediately.

I had this dream that I was on stage and everyone I knew was in the audience: the band, Paul, my mum and dad, even Lizzie Firestone and the boys from the garage who had come to our first gig. But when I tried to strum the first chords of the song, my fingers wouldn't move. And when I opened my mouth to sing, nothing came out. The crowd started booing and jeering. "Get a proper job." . . . "Learn to sing!" . . .

"Molly, Molly, Molly! . . . Molly!"

I woke up with a start to see Dean sitting on the edge of the bed.

"You looked like you were having a bad dream," he observed. "You were thrashing about like a maniac."

I ran a hand through my hair. "Yeah, I dreamed . . . Well, dreams never make sense, do they?"

I lay back on the pillow and watched the tense lines of his back as he sat there. He looked thinner, if that was possible. And I wondered if we actually knew each other at all. He was my first boyfriend—it seemed like such a ridiculous word to describe my relationship with Dean. *Boyfriend* suggested someone who picked you up at your house, made polite conversation with your parents, and took you out on dates to the cinema and the bowling alley and the really crap pub at the end of the pier, then snogged you at your front door. Dean and I had never done any of that.

"Do you mind if I get into bed?" he asked hesitantly. "It's a big bed, I won't touch you."

I frowned. "You're still allowed to touch me, if you want."

I heard him undressing and then felt the bed give as he got into it.

"Most of the time I feel like we're two people who're in a band who occasionally shag," he confessed. "You and me is so hard most of the time."

"I know," I sighed. I scooched over so I was spooning him,

and stroked his chest with my hand. "I bet you think I'm completely deranged."

"I don't think that, Moll," Dean protested. "It's just I never know what you're thinking. Paul told me that you want to quit."

My body tensed, and Dean rolled over so he was facing me. In the dim light, I could see his eyes squinting at me.

"Is it true?" he persisted.

I nodded. Then paused. "I just nodded, by the way," I said in a small voice.

I wasn't quite sure what Dean's reaction would be, but what he did next surprised me. He inched closer to me and kissed me more sweetly and tenderly than he'd ever done before, cupping my face in his hands and taking tiny baby sips from my mouth.

"Don't leave me," he whispered against my lips. "Please don't leave."

I smoothed my thumbs across the flat planes of his cheekbones. "Not leaving *you*, silly," I pointed out. "Leaving the band. There's a difference."

"But I can't do this without you," he insisted, and kissed me long and deep, wrapping his arms around my waist and pulling me closer.

We kissed slowly. Languidly. Hands exploring and reacquainting themselves with skin and curves and the little places that made us shudder and moan.

And when I was helpless with passion, Dean stilled and twined his fingers with mine.

"Say you won't go," he begged, beads of sweat decorating his forehead. "Say you'll stay. For me."

"Yes, yes, I'll stay," I gasped, and he began that beautiful, terrible dance again.

Afterward we slept in a tangle of arms and legs and sheets, and only woke up when the phone began to ring.

Dean stretched out with a groan and grunted into the receiver. "OK . . . yeah . . . yeah . . . No, it's fine . . . Really, it's cool . . . Yeah, no worries." He put down the phone down and collapsed back on to the mattress. "That was Frank," he announced. "We have to sound check. Paul's been kicking ass."

"Sound checking is good," I murmured sleepily. "And at least you didn't have to get your head kicked in this time."

Dean chuckled and tugged at my hair. "Yeah, but I don't think I can move."

But we had to move and shower and find clean clothes to wear on stage. I'd just pinned a flowery corsage onto the hip of my black flares and was wriggling into a pink chinese top when Dean came up behind me. Grabbing me around the waist, he maneuvered me in front of the mirror.

"We look good together," he said.

I stared back at our joint reflection. I saw a tall, dark-haired boy in jeans and a short-sleeved checked shirt, cuddling a girl who looked lost in his arms.

"What do you think?" he asked me.

"I think that this top clashes with my hair," I replied, and his face fell. "I'm just joking, Dean. We look OK. We're gonna be OK."

• • •

I'd played Dean "Missy and Me" during the sound check, and he'd been uncharacteristically effusive in his praise. He tidied up the chorus and sang it back to me, before commenting matter-of-factly, "This is about you and me, isn't it?"

"Write what you know," I stated simply, and he'd looked at his hands before changing the subject.

Yesterday had been the dark before the dawn, and today everything seemed brighter and certain. Something had given me my edge back. It might have been the sweet Dean lovin' or the decision to see this crazy pop-star thing through. Either way, I had a new sense of purpose—or as Jane said, "Molly's got her groove back," when I started playing the theme to *The Flintstones* halfway through the sound check.

That night, there were lots of ex-pats in the audience who'd turned up to check out the new Brit kids on the block, and KROQ (the local alternative radio station) had been playlisting us for weeks, so there were more cheers and less distracting mumbling through our set.

At the end of the show, the others walked off stage while the spotlight picked out me and Dean, and we performed an acoustic version of "Missy and Me," the song that would become my first and only Number One.

Another gig, another aftershow. Same old, same old. Paul networking his way across the room. Dean and me arm in arm, receiving a long line of people who wanted to tell us that we were the future of music. T and Tara playing one of their mammoth pinball tournaments, and Jane in the middle of the room, lit up like the fairy on top of the tree. White blond hair shining in the light, glitter dancing a trail across her skin, and her mouth stretched tight in a smile that never faded. I watched her dance through the crowd, her arms outstretched as she began to whirl faster and faster. As she moved in this encircling blur of denim and skin, the chatter and music seemed to disappear until all there was was Jane locked in her own private groove. Twisting and turning until she stopped. And slowly and gracefully collapsed to the floor.

I went in the ambulance with her. Paul was rushing around try-ing to make sure that no one took any photographs as Jane was lifted onto a gurney and carried down the stairs. I held her hand on the way to the hospital, but she was motionless as I stroked the blue cobweb of veins across her wrists.

We crashed through the Emergency Room doors, and then I stood and watched while she was suddenly beseiged on all sides by people in white coats and green scrubs. They lifted up her eyelids and pointed flashlights at her unresponsive pupils, stuck little tubes and sticky pads all over her so they could listen to the frenzied swooshing of her heart, and hooked her up to a drip.

"What's she taken?" they kept asking me.

But all I could do was shake my head blankly and say, "Pills. Some kind of pills, I think."

"How many did she take?"

"When did she take them?"

"Has she been drinking?"

When they started pumping this noxious black liquid down

her throat, someone tried to lead me out, but I stayed rooted to the spot as Jane began to cough and then retch.

There was a firm hand on my shoulder and a soft voice in my ear, and I was guided into a waiting room where the fluorescent lights burned my eyes.

I sat on a plastic chair for hours and thought how Jane had looked so small and still, lying on the trolley.

"I'll sort everything out."

I looked up to see Frank standing there. Good old Frank, who'd probably had more people OD on him than I had hair slides.

"Have the police spoken to you?" he wanted to know, and I shook my head.

"No, she's still being treated," I said, in a voice that seemed to come from miles away. "Do you think she's going to be all right?"

"Oh, she'll be fine," he replied breezily. "Look, this is really important. If the police want to ask you anything, get Paul to do the talking."

"But . . . but . . . but is Jane going to be *all right?*"

"Don't worry," Frank assured me, but he wouldn't look me in the eye. And I realized that he wasn't one of us, he was one of them.

I got a cab back from the hospital. The drived wanted to talk, but after I grunted noncommittally a few times, he got the message and left me to stare out of the window at the floodlit billboards and neon signs as they appeared out of the blackness. It wasn't enough to erase the picture of Jane with a tube stuck down her throat. Spending the night in an Emergency Room, watching your best friend get her stomach pumped, was never going to figure too highly in a travel guide.

I negotiated the hotel's revolving door and even managed the right words in the right order to get my room key. But it wasn't until I got into the lift and saw my ashen, bug-eyed reflection staring back at me in the mirror that I realized how distraught I actually was. The girl in the mirror looked like a disaster victim. But inside I was holding it together, going through the motions. 'Cause I knew that if I faltered, if I sighed, if I let one tear slip—I just might fall to pieces.

The lift doors were just closing when a Cuban-heeled boot suddenly wedged itself into the gap. They slid apart and the owner of the boot—a tall, skinny man who reeked of seediness like some guys reek of cheap aftershave—stepped into the lift, dragging a woman behind him.

He glanced at me once and turned to the woman. I studied them out of the corner of my eye. The hand he had wedged under the woman's arm seemed to be the only thing that was keeping her upright, as she tottered unsteadily and swung an open bag idly on loose fingers. She was wearing this rumpled chiffon dress that made her look like a child prostitute who'd just hit her forties, and as the man leaned into her I couldn't help but think that he looked like the pimp. I smiled to myself. But as she turned to hiss something at the man and I caught a proper glimpse of her, my stomach flipped.

It was Ruby X. My fearless, feminist, guitar-wielding hero. And she was barely there. Like an out-of-focus photograph. She and the man were arguing quietly. And that raspy, creosote-soaked voice that I'd spent hours listening to in the safety of my bedroom was slurred as she harangued the man about God knows what. I really tried not to look, but I couldn't help myself.

The man suddenly scrabbled at the lift panel and pressed a button, and she looked around wildly as if she'd only just realized where she was.

Our eyes didn't just meet, they collided. I've never believed all that rubbish about people expressing their emotions through their eyes. Yup, there are the basic signs, dilated pupils if it's dark, tears if they're racked with grief or chopping onions. But by and large, eyes tell you sweet nothing. But when I looked deep into her pale blue eyes with pupils the size of pinpricks, it was like looking at a car crash. Freeze frame. What my psychology teacher would have called a moment of total clarity. 'Cause as I looked, I saw the last year of my life in fast forward in front of me. The first gig at the community center. Dean giving me grief at the bar. The festival. Paul's office. The hotel rooms. The tour bus. Tara crying on the fire escape, and Jane lying on a trolley in a cubicle with a big black rubber tube in her mouth. But the images didn't just end there, they rushed on until the rock 'n' roll holocaust in front of me was simply my own reflection. I blinked and shook my head, and when I opened my eyes again, the lift was stopping and Ruby X and her companion were getting out.

Five floors later, the doors opened to let me make my escape. And as I stepped toward the opening, my foot trod on something. I bent down and picked up a lipstick that could only have fallen out of Ruby X's bag. It was a vampy, trampy red, flecked with glitter, and I idly wondered how much I'd get for it on eBay. I upended the tube to see what it was called and the words *Eve of Destruction* stared right back at me.

Ironic much?

When I got to Paul's hotel room, I paused and pulled my shoulders back, preparing to go into battle. Just as my hand was making a fist to knock on the door, I heard sounds coming from inside. Shouting voices. Paul and Dean's voices. And although my conscience was saying, "C'mon, Molly, move it along. Nothing to see here," there was also my bad-girl self who was much more persistent and kept hissing, "Just listen for a second. What harm can it do?" What harm indeed?

So I pressed my ear to the door. At first the sound was muffled. I was just about to knock when the argument started up again.

"This is killing me. Having to lie and pretend things are OK. She's not stupid."

"And neither are you. You went into this with your eyes wide open."

"It's wrong. God, it's so messed up."

"But she said she's staying? So no harm, no foul."

"And if she stays, it makes me happy. And if she goes, then I get to be the star."

"Look, Dean, *you* are the star. They'd be nothing without you. Yeah, that new song is better, but you're the one with the talent. But you need a pretty girl to draw in the press, otherwise you're just another bog-standard band with nothing new to offer."

"You're such a bastard."

"At least I'm not the one sleeping with her . . ."

"This isn't about us sleeping together . . ."

"Think of it this way—you get the girl *and* the fame. It's a sweet setup."

"And you get me doing your dirty work for you. This thing with Jane—it's going to get Molly freaking out again."

"Jane's out, I told you. I'll deal with Molly, put the fear of God into her again, and then you can be around to pick up the pieces. Believe me, you're getting the better end of the deal."

"If she knew—"

"Well, she's not going to find out unless you tell her . . ."

What do you do when you find out the boy you love is a big fat liar? A treacherous, evil scumbag in league with someone who's already threatened you with death and legal proceedings?

You go to reception, pick up the spare key to your room so the treacherous, evil scumbag won't be able to get in, then lock the door, sit on the toilet, and think coldly and calculatedly about your Plan B.

That's what you *should* do. What I actually did was start banging on the door and screeching like a foul-mouthed harpie from some freaky hell dimension. The door suddenly swung open and I fell against it, with my fist still raised.

Paul took a couple of cautious steps away from where I stood, red faced and panting. Dean was leaning against the desk, his mouth and eyes three perfect circles of horror.

"You utter bastards," I screamed. "You set me up! I gave you my heart and you've stomped on it with your horrid boy feet. I hate you!"

Anger is like feeling sick; it comes rising through your stomach and out of your mouth, and you can do nothing but let it take you over. I shouted and ranted and swore and clenched my fists. I kicked Paul's suitcase so hard that it skidded against the wall and burst open, spilling out Calvin Klein boxer shorts and Paul Smith shirts in a variety of pastel colors. Paul and Dean were still frozen like a pair of pox-ridden statues as I stumbled after the suitcase, fell to my knees, and started ripping whatever items of clothing I could get hold of. With my bare hands. I was like that girl from *Crouching Tiger, Hidden Dragon* if she'd got really pissed off.

"You treat me like some stupid toy, and Jane could be lying dead on a hospital trolley, and the only thing you two care about is making money. And it's dirty, it messes everything it touches," I spat out, tearing the arms off a powder-blue shirt. "I hate you! I hate you! I hate you!"

The only sounds in the room were my voice rising and rising toward the "hysterical" setting and the ripping of material. Still they said and did nothing. But when I ran out of clothes to destroy and picked up the suitcase and tried to hurl it out of the closed windows, I felt a pair of arms snake round me and try to hold me back. I knew it was Dean, I could smell the coconut wax in his hair. I tried to swivel round and thrashed my limbs wildly, hoping to break his grip, but he was pulling me to my feet.

"Stop it, Molly," he growled. "You're behaving like a maniac."

I gave a furious, wordless shriek as he yanked me round so I was facing Paul, who was looking at the tattered remnants of the contents of his suitcase with disbelief. I collapsed my legs out so Dean and I nearly toppled onto the floor. But he dragged me toward a chair and pushed me down into it, the hard sting of his fingers on my shoulders, keeping me firmly in my place.

"Do you ever think what it says about you that you'll sleep with a girl just because your manager has told you to?" I asked him in a cold voice, tilting my head back so I could see my words hit him.

"I slept with you because I've been in love with you ever since the first day we met," Dean choked out, and then he was coming round me and crouching down so I could see the tears trickling down his cheeks. "I love you, and if you knew how hard it's been—"

"You want me to feel sorry for you because all the lying and scheming behind my back turned out to be more difficult than you realized?" I spluttered. "You are unbelievable."

"I never asked him to shag you," Paul suddenly said, abandoning his silent contemplation of his wrecked wardrobe and leaning against the door. "You'll remember that I was against the idea right from the first moment you started pawing at each other."

We both turned to glare at him.

"So who's the star then, Paul?" I purred. "Is it me, like you've been claiming ever since you smarmed your way into my parents' front room? Or is it Dean, and am I just—what was it—'the pretty girl to draw in the press'?"

Paul wouldn't look either of us in the eye. He was pale underneath his St. Tropez tan, and his fingers drummed noiselessly against his thighs.

"I was just trying to motivate you both," he said eventually. "Bit of friendly competition, that's all."

"Arsehole."

"Wanker."

Paul's eyes narrowed and he pushed himself away from the wall and walked to the door. "Out, both of you," he ordered tonelessly, turning the handle.

I jumped up from the chair and kicked it backward so it thudded against the desk before toppling over.

"What do you do for an encore?" Paul asked nastily. "Going to use your skinny little arms to try and chuck the telly out of the window?"

"Why would I do that when I can think of much better ways to hurt you and your precious balance sheets," I hissed, flouncing over to the open door and making sure that I knocked into Paul hard on my way out.

Dean followed me.

"You want to know who the real star of the band is?" Paul called after us. "It's *me*. You owe me everything, you tragic pair of little wanna-bes."

Dean whirled round and swore fluently and graphically back. But Paul was already slamming the door.

I started running toward the lift, but Dean was faster. As he picked up speed, his fingertips brushed my arm and he managed to curl his hand around my wrist.

"God! Molly, will you just stop and listen to me?" he begged, trying to wrap himself around me again.

I pushed him away. "What could you possibly say that I'd want to hear?" I demanded, slapping his lying arms away.

"I love you," he pleaded.

And it broke my heart into a thousand tiny pieces. Because it was only now, when I knew that I could never stand to be near him again, that he was telling me what I'd always wanted to hear.

"I don't love you," I lied, and listened appalled to my stupid voice like it belonged to someone else. "You were just convenient. I shagged you and it meant that I didn't have to fight off a whole bunch of other losers who wanted to be able to tell their friends that they'd had me. And I'm glad that this whole stupid lie is over."

He let me go then. Stumbled away from me like I'd just given him a week to live. His face crumpled and he staggered backward, as I turned and walked away from him.

I ran back to my room, eyes blinded with tears, and made a long-distance call that I probably wouldn't have made if I'd sought legal advice.

Afterward, I felt purged. Squeaky clean and shiny on the inside. Ready for any crap that Paul wanted to sling at me.

Then I went to bed and fell into a deep and dreamless sleep as soon as my head moved toward the pillow.

But the strange thing about an apocalyptic night before is that the morning after is always going to be anticlimactic. When I entered the breakfast room with a rumbling belly and the tiniest flickering of fear that Paul might get security to throw me out, there they were eating bacon and eggs and acting like nothing untoward had happened.

Tara waved at me. "We're over here," she called. "I've already ordered for you. One fry-up on its way," she added as I pulled out the remaining empty chair and gave her a bewildered look.

I glanced over at Paul and Dean, who were sitting opposite

each other. But Dean was head down in a bowl of Lucky Charms, and Paul gave me the briefest of smiles and carried on the conversation he was having with his mobile phone.

"You look all serious," Tara remarked, and then her face perked up. "Oh, Jane! Don't worry, Paul's phoned the hospital and she's going to be OK."

"Good," I mumbled, and shook out my napkin for want of something better to do. "So . . . Y'know that I'm—"

"I've told them about last night," Paul interrupted me quickly. "About your little temper tantrum. Just as well that we're all taking a holiday once this bloody tour is finally over."

"B-b-b-but that's not what . . ." I stammered, and then shut my mouth. Better to say nothing until I discovered the full extent of Paul's spin-doctoriness. "Whatever," I snapped, in a tone that would have got me instant grounding if I was back home. But I wasn't at home. I was in a Marriott Hotel in L.A. and everyone was stuffing down their breakfasts and not paying much attention to the nuances and inflections in my voice.

It got even stranger after that. We had a whole day off so we could do promo, but Paul had canceled every single interview under the flimsy excuse that we should all go sight-seeing as a fun, bonding experience.

I'd have rather had my head shaved and intricate tribal patterns carved into my scalp, but I found myself getting in a people carrier and being driven to Santa Monica.

As we walked past the buskers on the promenade that led to the pier, I began to wonder if I'd had my drink spiked last night and everything that had happened after we came off stage had been some freaky hallucination.

Dean bought me candy floss and we ambled through the fun fair, his hand tightly clutching mine as he kept furtively whispering in my ear, "It will be all right, honestly. Everything will be all right, I'll make things better." Every time I tried to pull my hand free or argue with him, he'd cast frantic glances at the others, and T or Tara would suddenly be at my side talking at twice the speed of light about absolutely nothing. Paul was a shadowy presence behind us, despite the fierce glare of the sun, mumbling into his phone and piercing holes into my back with his eyes.

The day from Bizarreville continued with Paul finally admitting to himself that he couldn't stand the sight of us (well, me) and disappearing into a cab, still surgically attached to his phone.

The four of us had lunch in a cafe by the water, and Dean watched me eat strawberries with the same kind of rapt fascination as if I was painting the ceiling of the Sistine Chapel. And when I took off my trainers and socks to paddle in the Pacific, he said that he envied the waves that were kissing my feet. I think it was a line from a song, and I came out of my funk long enough to hiss that he didn't have an original idea in his head. He said, "Well, you have enough for both of us."

I have pictures that we took in a photo booth that day: T, Tara, Dean, and me all crammed together. I'm sitting on Dean's lap, my face grim and unsmiling, like I'm in a police station having my mug shot taken. But in the last frame my face is in profile, as

I reach up to look at Dean with an expression on my face that suggests he might possibly be on crack. He looks like he's in love with me.

It might seem strange that I didn't run from the enforced day of fun, screaming at the top of my little lungs. But to tell you the truth, I was saving up all the seconds I still had left with Dean, so I could stash them in a tiny box in the corner of my heart and leaf through them on those dark nights when sleep was a long time coming. So I walked and I talked and I window-shopped, and I wondered what lies Paul had told T and Tara, because they were acting like I was going to throw a hissy fit at any moment and they had to be there to jolly me out of it. I struggled to maintain an indifferent kind of dignity, but, as usual, it came out as a childish sulkiness. I could feel my lower lip jutting out in the biggest pout this side of the *Guinness Book of World Records* and my eyebrows pulling together in a permanent scowl.

It was a relief to get to the club where we were playing our last gig of the tour. Paul was waiting for us with a short, pink-haired guy carrying a guitar case. Paul's eyes narrowed as he saw me and Dean come in first, my hand tightly clutched in his, and my face stony as he tried to nuzzle my neck. It was a pretty nauseating sight, I suppose.

"This is Tito," Paul said tersely. "He's standing in for Jane."

"Hi," said Tito, holding up a hand in greeting.

"Is Jane still in hospital?" I asked Paul in a monotone.

I'd tried to ring that morning, but all that they'd tell me was that she was stable and not up to visitors.

"She's fine," Paul replied, his eyes shifting away from me to rest on a point about three inches above my head. "But Tito will be doing the last show. He's the best bassist in the city. He's played with Beck, you know."

Tito shrugged as if it was no big deal. He was so laid-back that I thought he'd fall over.

"And Jane?" I inquired icily.

"Jane will come back home with us, and then she needs to . . . Well, she needs some specialist help, doesn't she? You have to see that."

"I do," I agreed, and wondered for the billionth time why I'd ever imagined that Paul was my savior.

Dean squeezed my hand and then let go. "So we should probably run through the set with Tito," he suggested. "Most of our songs are really simple."

"Hey, man, no worries," said Tito. "Never met a bass line I couldn't manage."

"I'll leave you to it, then," Paul interrupted smoothly, and touched me lightly on the shoulder.

I managed to restrain myself from flinching and arched an eyebrow at him. "What?"

"I'm sorry about Jane," he said. And when I saw the rueful look on his face—regret tinged with something that might have been guilt . . . or just a trick of the light—I realized he was telling the truth.

"Thank you," I said simply, and then turned away as the club promoter tapped me on the arm and handed me a fax of a press clipping that I'd been waiting for all day.

• • •

So, forty-one shows done, one to go. I stood at the side of the stage, watching Tim tape our set lists to the floor, and felt the familiar flutter of butterflies in my stomach that told me we were going to go out with an ungodly roar.

I was wearing my mum's wedding dress again. I'd forgotten that I'd packed it, but I found it scrunched into a corner of my suitcase. I'd dug it out and scrounged an iron from the hotel housekeeper.

Someone had told Tito that flowers were my big thing, and after the sound check (where he'd nailed every song after one take and left us feeling intimidated as hell), he'd produced a single pink gardenia and presented it to me. "For letting me share your big night," he'd said, and almost produced a facial expression when I'd ruffled his hair.

Our intro tape was playing. We always went on to the theme from *Buffy* and stood there with stony faces, like it was a perfectly appropriate intro song.

As the feedback squealed, signaling our cue, I turned to Tara and lifted her head so I could look into her eyes. Then I kissed her slowly on the lips. She pulled away and touched her mouth with her fingers, like she couldn't believe what I'd just done.

"Don't hate me too much," I whispered in her ear, picked up my guitar, and stepped center stage.

We were gods that night. Gods from some heavenly dimension where guitars and charity-shop keyboards had replaced harps and angelic choirs. I let the music love me and I loved it right back. I dedicated "I Can See My Life From Here" to "Jane—who's not here but in our hearts, and to Ruby X—for showing me the way." And when I introduced "Missy and Me," I said, "This is a song for anyone who's ever been lonely." As I sang, the words came from a place so deep inside me that it was almost a struggle to give them life. I killed my demons with my pink guitar. And I laughed when a girl from the audience jumped on stage and quietly and patiently stood by my side as I sang "Hello Kitty Speedboat", kissed me on the cheek, and then jumped back into the crowd.

We finished our set with a cover of the Beatles' "Here Comes the Sun," and as we stopped playing, I looked round at Tara and T—and yup, even Dean. They smiled and nodded at me, and I couldn't believe that they had no idea what was coming. It was so obvious. The audience were clapping and shouting for an encore when I stepped up to the mic and tapped it with my finger. The applause died away, and there was an expectant murmur as I smiled.

"Thank you for coming to our last American show," I said in a voice that only wavered slightly. "This is my last ever show, and I'm glad I got to share it with you. We *were* The Hormones. And now . . . and . . . now we're not. Good night."

And then I gently placed my guitar on the floor and walked out of the spotlight.

I'd barely made it to the wings before I was nose to nose with Paul, who was incandescent with rage and waving a copy of a fax that looked *very* familiar.

• • •

--- EXCLUSIVE! ---
GOOD GOLLY MISS MOLLY

Hormones lead singer quits band

As WE WERE GOING TO PRESS LAST NIGHT, *HOT LIST* Deputy Editor, Spike Gunn, received an emotional phone call from Hormones lead singer, Molly Montgomery, who exclusively revealed that she was leaving the band after their current U.S. tour.

'I started the band because I was in love with music and the way a song could touch me,' Molly confessed from her hotel room in L.A. 'But if I stay, I'll end up hating it.'

Molly also revealed her disenchantment with the band's management company, Monster Management, and Paul Blake, who personally manages the Hormones.

'I don't think he's said an honest word to me from the day I met him,' Molly told us. 'He's threatened to kill me and sue me for breaching a contract I was manipulated into signing on the evening of my eighteenth birthday, when he'd been plying me with alcohol for hours.'

Molly fought back tears throughout the duration of the call, often sounding extremely overwrought. 'I was told what to sing, what to wear, what to say in interviews,' she went on. 'Until I didn't recognise the person I was being forced to become.'

Although Molly wouldn't confirm reports that Hormones bassist, Jane Fabian, had been rushed to hospital earlier that night with a suspected drug overdose, she would admit to a relationship with lead guitarist, Dean Speed. 'We got together at Christmastime,' said Molly, her voice catching. 'I loved him, but I realise now that Dean was only with me because it was a good way to get more control of the band that I started.'

Before she rang off, Molly assured us that she'd perform the last date of the U.S. tour at L.A.'s famous Whisky A Go-Go, before returning to her hometown of Southport for some much-needed downtime. 'I want to stay in bed for at least a month, and I hope I don't get sued,' she said.

The Hot List tried to reach Hormones manager, Paul Blake, for a quote, but were told by hotel staff that there was no reply from his room.

For the full interview, see next week's *Hot List*.

Paul was literally frothing at the mouth in his eagerness to exact punishment. "I am going to sue the living daylights out of you," he screamed, pinning me against the wall. "Get back on the stage and make it right."

"You can't make it right," I growled. "It will never be right again. I'm done. I'm finished. And before you start threatening me with legal action, you already know that I've done an interview with *The Hot List*. A candid, no-holds-barred interview that will be out on Wednesday explaining in great detail how you lied and manipulated me and exhorted me into signing a contract."

"You little bitch," Paul shouted, shoving me even harder into the wall, his face red with anger. "I'm going to kill you!"

But he wasn't going to kill me, and he wasn't even going to keep banging me against a hard surface, because T suddenly grabbed him around the waist and pulled him off me.

"Back off!" Tara snarled at Paul, stepping between him and me while I walked on semi-shaky legs toward the exit. "Let her go. We don't need her, anyway."

"Molly! Come back here and stop being so bloody stupid," I heard Paul call out.

I half turned to see him shrugging out of T's grasp and trying to smooth out the creases in his suit. "I'm out of here," I said. "My lawyers will be in touch."

It was a great exit line. Just the right amount of feistiness and grit. I could still hear Paul spluttering and swearing as I walked out of the stage door and into the balmy breeze of L.A. at night. I found myself in an alley at the back of the club and leaned against the wall to look up at the stars all twinkling away like they didn't have a care in the world.

The door opened and Dean stepped out, clutching my guitar.

"Hey," I said, like we'd just bumped into each other in the middle of the street.

Dean reached out and tucked a stray lock of hair behind my ear. I stroked his hand for a second and then twisted my lips in a fair approximation of a smile. He looked deep into my eyes with a confused look on his face, like he was trying to search for a particularly difficult crossword clue.

"OK, Dean, you have to speak," I said after a few moments. "All this staring and silence is beginning to freak me out."

"You've made your point," he finally said. "Now come back to the band and come back to me."

"It's over," I sighed. "For the first time in a year, I'm absolutely certain that I'm doing the right thing."

"You wouldn't know the right thing if it bit you on the arse," Dean snapped. "You can't just walk out."

"I just have," I pointed out. "Weren't you paying attention back there?"

"But I love you," Dean insisted, trying to thrust the guitar into my hands. I refused to take it.

"It's not enough," I told him gently. "But what I said to you last night wasn't true. I did love you, I loved you passionately. And you betrayed me in the worst possible—"

"Molly! Is it true? I can't believe you quit the band like that. It's so sad."

I looked around to see a small throng of kids standing behind us.

"It's true," I muttered, and as I walked toward them, they stepped back to let me through.

I got to the mouth of the alley and I turned round to steal one last look at Dean. Our eyes met for a second, and then he turned away and shoved my pink guitar at a girl who was gazing at him in wordless admiration. "You can have this," I heard him say. "She won't be needing it anymore."

It was the end of the fairy tale, and even though Cinderella didn't have anything useful like a purse or credit card or a glass slipper she could pawn for a plane ticket home, she could still remember how to use a phone.

"This is the international operator. Will you accept a collect call from Molly Montgomery?"

"Molly? But she's in L.A.! Yes, I'll accept. Molly?"

"Hi, Dad. It's me."

That was the end of it really. And the start of something else. The Very Cherry hair is gone, replaced by a honey blond color that makes me look younger or older depending on the light. I'm at university, studying art history, and for five minutes I was a legend on campus. But eventually the black-clad girls and the arrogant boys who wanted to bed a rock star and brag about it in the student-union bar got fed up with asking me, "Didn't you used to be famous?" I'd always smile and reply, "You've got me confused with someone else."

I see Jane all the time. After rehab, she moved to London too. She wants to be a fashion designer when she finally grows up. And the biggest shock is that she's going out with a shy art student who blushes when she walks into the room and puts love letters in her lunch box. She reckons it's the real thing. And who am I to argue? We're in a band again too, called Duckie—and lots of men in suits with big checkbooks started sniffing round again. Big whoop. Instead, we signed to a tiny, teeny label who can just about afford to take us out for coffee, and we write songs about what we watched on telly the other night. Oh yeah, and dark-haired boys who steal your heart away.

I don't talk to the others. Those awful months when I first left the band and hid from the constant ringing of the telephone by shutting the bedroom door and heaping the covers over my head were made worse by the interviews that they gave to the music papers. Paul gave a press conference a few days after the end of the American tour where he pontificated at great length about my various shortcomings: "Molly just didn't have that in-definable star quality. At best, she'll be remembered as a tiny footnote in the book of women in rock." He really must stop tak-ing those arsehole lessons. T told them that I was "a stuck-up princess who would never speak to me." Tara insisted that "she got one taste of fame and became absolutely impossible." It hurt. God, how it hurt.

And then there was Dean. Oddly enough he never bad-mouthed me to the press. In fact, he gave an interview to my old friend Spike Gunn recently and said, "I can't talk about Molly because of the whole legal thing. I just hope that she's happy and she doesn't hate me too much."

Sometimes in the dead of night, when I've been dreaming of white horses and helter-skelters, I'm woken up by the ringing of the phone. There's never any answer when I pick it up, but once I heard Sandrine say crossly, "Dean, who the freaking hell are you calling at this time of night?" She's in the band now, singing Dean's songs and pouting furiously every time there's a camera within a five-mile radius. And in the two years since I left, they've become really famous. They spend most of their time in L.A. now and hang out with young Hollywood actors. I think there's even talk of them doing a movie.

I hear all this from Charles, my lawyer. Paul was true to his word and has been dragging my sorry self through the courts as he sues me for breach of contract. Then we countersue. It's a whole suing thing. I don't even want to think about the legal fees I'm racking up, but Charles says that I can pay him back when we win. *If* we win.

But there was someone else in this story. Someone that there wouldn't be a story without. Ruby X died eighteen months ago of a drug overdose. Everyone acted surprised that she'd been struggling with heroin addiction for years. Not me. And though there was talk of a suicide, no one could find a note. The night I heard that she'd left without leaving a forwarding address, I put on Ruby's first album, *Bitch Goddess*, and lit a candle to speed her on her way to somewhere better. And cried my heart out for the both of us.

A week after I'd heard the news on the radio, I got a huge package forwarded to me from Charles's office. I was kinda hoping that it was a few million quid in used notes from a well-wisher, but when I tore through the paper and string and cardboard, I found Ruby's gold, custom-made Rickenbacker guitar. Tucked into the strings was a piece of paper. When I unfolded it, the smell of violets hung heavy in the air. She'd written:

Dear Molly,

You remember me from the elevator all those months ago, don't you? You looked at me, and all I could see was the girl I used to be. It made me feel sad. It made me want to gather you up, sweet baby, so no one could hurt you like they hurt me.

I'm tired now. So bone-weary, bloodshot-eyed, skin stretched tight. And I think it's better to burn than fade away.

You be strong, honey, and look after my guitar (I heard you lost yours) and promise me that you'll keep rocking. Yeah, keep on rocking...

Lots of love,
Ruby
X

It's weird, but despite everything that's happened to me, I still believe that you can write a song and change someone's life forever.

Turn the page for a sneak peek
at Sarra Manning's new novel

PRETTY THINGS...

Brie is in love with Lancôme Juicy Tubes, Louis Vuitton accessories, and Charlie, her gay best friend.

Charlie is in love with 1960s pop art, 1980s teen movies, and serial heartbreaker Walker.

Walker has ever only been in love with his VW Bug, until he meets Daisy.

And **Daisy** is too busy hating everyone to know what love is.

This is a story about kissing people you shouldn't, breaking hearts because there's nothing to watch on telly, and falling in love and off your heels.

"She's my best friend, certainly not the average girl."

Charlie

I think I've spent roughly one third of my entire life in Brie's bedroom. I've seen her walls covered in Paddington Bear wallpaper. I've seen the walls covered in pictures of Westlife (which, quite frankly, I still have nightmares about), and I helped paint the walls the current fetching shade of Pink Sequin Editions Indian Summer Flat Matte, which isn't as garish as it sounds. It was also my idea to paint the ceiling midnight blue with lots of little stars sprinkled all over it. I spend a lot of time lying in, on, or around Brie's bed, so I like having something pretty to look at.

I like sleeping with Brie; she never hogs the covers and she keeps her elbows to herself. I even have a drawer here full of T-shirts and clean pants and a spare jar of moisturizer, which simples things up so much.

Brie was snoring very gently and delicately when I woke up

this morning. And when I got back from the bathroom, she was still asleep. Which wasn't a huge surprise. Loves her sleep, does Brie. I pulled on my Belle and Sebastian T-shirt, walked across the room, and looked out the window.

The pavement was already glistening; bumblebees, fat and stupid from too much pollen, buzzed lazily round the lavender bush in her front garden. It was going to be another of those hot summer days when the air seems to shimmer with possibilities. So I didn't know why Brie was wrapped round her flowery duvet like it was the dead of winter.

I tugged gently on the chocolate-brown hair that was all that was visible of her.

"Hey! Sleepy girl! You need to get your arse out of bed," I whispered, leaning down to uncover her ear. "If we're late for the first day, I'm going to claim ownership of the iPod for the whole week."

She gave a tiny, delicate moan and burrowed deeper under the duvet.

It was time for Plan B. "Okay, I'm going to rifle through your underwear drawer, find your grungiest knickers, and sell them on eBay."

The covers were sloughed off with an indignant squeak. "Ewww, that's gross," she mumbled. "And I don't have any grungy knickers."

Brie emerging from sleep is like watching a flower slowly unfurl its petals. She stretched slowly, pink tongue poking out of her mouth as she yawned, her hands curled into fists as she batted the air like a playful kitten.

"What color am I?" she asked eagerly, kicking back her duvet and kneeling to investigate.

I looked at the pale thighs emerging from her boxer shorts.

"Well," I said consolingly. "You're a sort of clotted cream color, and yesterday you were more of a semi-skimmed milk. The sheets, on the other hand, are seriously bronzed."

Brie looked up from dismayed contemplation of her legs and stared at the fake-tan stains on the sheets as if she wasn't quite sure how they got there.

"Well, I'm not going to that drama club thingy," she announced simply, lying back down and pulling the duvet back over her head. "I'm meant to have a tan! I can't act if I'm not looking good." The last two sentences were muffled, and then the Brie-shaped hump started shaking slightly, and I knew she was crying.

Sometimes I worry about how Brie will cope when something genuinely catastrophic happens instead of the usual crap that she deems weep-worthy. If Timberlake, her cat, died, or she found out she had six weeks to live, or her hair fell out, she'd probably have to have a Prozac drip installed.

It really wasn't the right time for Brie to be having one of her regularly scheduled weepathons. I'd begged and cajoled and pleaded to get her to sign up for the summer drama workshop that was starting today. Getting her through the auditions, getting her to *pass* her audition, had taken years off my tender, young life. Because no way, no how, was I going to spend another summer watching daytime TV and eating crisps while Brie watched me eating crisps and occasionally snuck one into her mouth when she thought I wasn't looking.

Getting Brie out of bed and in the mood to kick some drama-workshop butt wasn't just a matter of necessity. It was a matter of life and death. Like that bit in a movie when there's a bomb with a ticking clock attached to it, and it's counting down sixty seconds, and the guy who knows whether the red or the blue wire should be cut isn't going to talk. Down-and-dirty tactics was all that I had left.

"Okay, don't come," I said, like I didn't care in the slightest, while bouncing up and down on her bed in a manner that I knew was going to piss her off. "It's not my problem if you have nothing else in life and you fail your certificate in Beauty Therapy Sciences and have to end up pretending that you're between jobs when really you're working in a call center or worse! Yeah! You're working in Burger King, and the grease is clogging up your pores, and you can't afford proper products anymore, so all the shine has gone from your hair because you're using supermarket own-brand shampoo."

It worked. There was an anguished moan from the bed-clothes, and then Brie was falling out of bed to shoot me a baleful glare before disappearing into the bathroom.

It would be at least three-quarters of an hour before she was ready, so I turned on her ceramic hair straighteners and headed down to the kitchen.

Brie's house smells of furniture polish and Glade PlugIns with an overpowering top note of Dunhill International cigarettes and Gucci Rush, courtesy of her mum. The smell is only temporarily relieved when you're in Brie's room, which stinks of fake tan and Anna Sui Sweet Dreams.

Everything in Brie's house is white and gold to match Linda, who vacuums three times a day. You have the audacity to eat a bag of crisps while you're waiting for Brie to get off the telephone, and there she is trying to trip you up with her Dyson.

Linda looked up when I walked into the kitchen and waved

the coffeepot at me enticingly. "Morning, sweetie. You're looking particularly handsome today. Pity you couldn't find a hairbrush, though." I could tell that Linda had only had one cup of coffee. Usually she's not quite so laid-back.

I kissed her on the cheek, grabbed a mug from the cupboard, and sat down at the kitchen table, where Henry, Brie's angelic-looking younger brother, was shoveling cornflakes into his gaping maw. This prevented him from sticking his tongue out or giving me the finger, which is what I usually get from him by way of a greeting. Little shit.

Mr. Brie, or Dave as I never call him, was cowering behind the *Daily Mail* as usual and giving the appearance of a man on the edge of a nervous breakdown.

"It's Charlie," Linda announced unnecessarily. Mr. Brie moved his paper aside to give me a nod, but Henry didn't even bother to look up from spraying milk and cereal all over the table. He did manage to reach under the table and kick me extra hard on the shin, though.

At least Linda gave me a cup of extra-strong coffee before we embarked on our usual conversation.

"So, how are you, Charlie?" (She has this really annoying habit of saying my name at the end of every sentence like she has to remind herself who she's talking to.)

"I'm fine, Linda. How are you?"

"Well, I wish I could say I was fine, but I'm not, Charlie. How's your mum?"

"She's okay."

"So you and Brie were home very late last night, Charlie. I hope you gave her a chance to meet other boys, because she'll meet someone else, you know, and then you'll be wishing that you'd been more thrusting and dynamic and grabbed her when you had the chance," Linda said brightly, tapping her cigarette into the ashtray, which was nestled next to the milk jug on the kitchen table. Even a hardened smoker like myself winced at Linda's relaxed attitude to smoking near fresh dairy.

Mr. Brie snorted a couple of times at this damning indictment of my girl-getting skills, because his gaydar is far more evolved than his wife's, which is actually quite disturbing when you think about it.

"I'm not really into girls, Linda." Which she knew damn well. "But if I was, then I'm sure me and Brie would be picking out china patterns and saving for our honeymoon. And anyway you must be secretly relieved that I don't have dishonorable intentions toward your daughter."

"Hmm, you say that, Charlie, but I'm sure if the right girl were to come along, you'd stop all this nonsense. It's just a shame that Brie isn't pretty enough to change your mind."

Which of course was Brie's cue to trip into the kitchen just in time to hear her mother's judgment on her looks.

For a second her face collapsed. Her perfect little smudge of a nose wrinkled up, and her green eyes went cloudy. There was even a slight lip tremble until her features righted themselves into their eternal loveliness. I didn't know what Linda was on because, really, Brie is ridiculously gorgeous.

Brie shook her newly straightened hair out of her eyes, blinked a couple of times, and then sidled nearer so she could give me a good-morning kiss.

"I don't suppose you woke me up too early, 'cause I haven't had breakfast yet, you know?" She was already moving past me to investigate the contents of the fridge.

"No, I'm on time, and you're late. Again. Can we go?"

But was Brie concerned with being hideously late for our

first day of drama group? Yeah, right! In the Brie-verse, there were far more important things to worry about.

"There's no bacon or eggs or sausages," she whined at Linda with a wounded look on her face. "I have to have a fry-up for breakfast. You know I'm not doing carbs."

Linda tapped out another cigarette from the packet and knocked the filter tip against her frosted pink talons. "You shouldn't eat all that fatty food, you'll get porky. I'm sure you've put on weight since last week."

And then Brie looked down in horror at her thin little legs in their Diesel jeans, and Linda's work here was done.

I got up—careful not to scrape back my chair on the newly waxed kitchen floor—then grabbed my bag and Brie.

"Get something to eat now, and then we're going," I said in my most "don't mess with me, bitch" voice, the one I use exclusively to chivvy Brie along.

There was a sorrowful sigh, which would have made a lesser being break down in tears. I just gave her a flinty-eyed look and waved my watch in her face until she grabbed a bag of salt-and-vinegar crisps from the cupboard and a can of Diet Coke from the fridge.

"Well, bye bye, sweetie," Linda said, and I wasn't entirely sure which one of us she was speaking to. "Break a leg or something."

Brie muttered something that may or may not have been "bitch" under her breath and picked up her Louis Vuitton Murakami Cherry Blossom bag from the stairs as I followed her out.

We stepped out into the blinding sunlight and simultaneously reached for our sunglasses. Brie was studying the nutritional information on the back of the crisps packet, her lips moving as she sounded out the words. "Seventeen point three grams of carbs," I heard her mutter. "I should be able to digest them by seven tonight."

I reached around to give her waist a comforting squeeze. "Linda has issues on her issues, right? And she only says mean stuff about you because she can't handle that you're cute and hot and she's thundering toward menopause."

Brie tucked her arm into mine and pulled her Von Dutch baseball cap down so she wouldn't freckle. "But, Charlie, you would tell me if I was fat, wouldn't you?"

Brie was wearing tight, low-rider jeans, which showed off her practically concave stomach to its best advantage. Then there was the floaty, gauzy top, which may have been a pocket handkerchief in another life. "Brie, you are not fat. You are as far from fat as it's possible to be. Now shut the fuck up because this conversation is getting really boring." And there was a God because she shut up and actually started walking, giving us an outside chance of catching the bus and getting to Camden before ten.

"We haven't had the postmortem about last night," I reminded her as we got to the bus stop, and she squinted up at the indicator board to see how long it would be before the bus chugged into view.

Brie didn't answer for a while because she was digging around in her bag. But eventually she pulled out her Lancôme Juicy Tube in Marshmallow, slicked it over her lips, and answered me. "There wasn't a single guy in there who knew how to dress." Pause, while she gave me a Significant Look from under her lashes. "Not like you."

"That's because I'm gay, sweetie. Being a style icon is all part of my genetic coding."

"I wish you weren't gay."

"I wish that you didn't wish that I wasn't gay."

Brie and I have this conversation at least five times every day. I love her, she's my best friend, but even if I *was* straight or she was a boy, I'm not entirely sure that we'd go out or ever have one frenzied night of passion on her Calvin Klein bed linen.

I'm an indie/emo hybrid. All my T-shirts have faded in the wash, and I cut my hair with nail scissors and bleach the ends when I get bored. I own three pairs of Converse All Star low-tops, each one more battered than the last, and I bite my nails. Though I do have an incredibly chiseled jawline, if you happened to be comparing me to, say, someone who didn't have a jawline at all. And if I was straight, which I'm not, the kind of girl I'd want to fall wildly and passionately and madly in love with would be Brody from the Distillers.

Brie, meanwhile, is a pastel-colored princess who'd love to get me into Gucci anything and has offered many times to actually pay for me to get my hair properly highlighted. She also has a disturbing tendency to dress like a footballer's wife.

Which is not to say she doesn't appreciate my not-so-inconsiderable charms. I'm very pretty, in a manly kind of way.

"Ooooh, Charlie, you have the longest, fluffiest boylashes I've ever seen," she's fond of saying, before getting huffy because she has to apply two coats of Eyelure Kiss Me Mascara to get the same effect.

As we got on the bus and I gave the driver two tickets because Brie never manages to get it together to buy the prepaid books, she turned to me, mouthed an apology, and smiled.

"I don't know what I'd do without you," she murmured,

before heading for the stairs, and I realized that even though she annoyed the hell out of me and there was no reason for our friendship whatsoever, I couldn't think of another person in this world that I'd want to be my best friend.

The ride into Camden was pretty uneventful. Mostly we hoped that the fat goth boy who'd stunk of patchouli oil and glommed on to us when we'd auditioned hadn't made the final cut.

"It took me forever to get the stink out of my hair," Brie remembered with a shudder. "I hope everyone's nice. And cute. I need cute boys this summer. Lots of them."

"I hear you," I said feelingly. "One cute boy for you and one for me. We could double-date." I rubbed her shoulder. "So, honey, you ready for your close-up?"

Brie suddenly squinched up her face as if she was in great pain. "Shit!" she exclaimed. "I forgot about the whole acting thing. That weird woman in charge, she's going to expect us to act, isn't she?"

I nodded gravely. " 'Fraid so. I think it's pretty much a pre-requisite of a drama group."

"Don't use long words, they give me a headache." Brie looked at her half-eaten bag of crisps and then violently threw them down the bus, earning her glares from a couple of grannies who didn't appreciate getting crisp crumbs in their blue rinses. "Oh God, I feel sick. I don't want everyone staring at me. Why did I let you talk me into this?"

Knowing very well that she's the biggest drama queen this side of wherever Paris Hilton lives, I didn't really waste much time consoling Brie. Instead I clasped her hand in mine and gave it a little shake.

"Listen, Brie," I said urgently. "We're going to make a pact."

"What kind of pact? I'm not spitting on your hand or nothing 'cause that's really unhygienic."

I swear to God, I have the patience of a saint. "We are going to swear on our iPod that we will do everything in our power, short of illegal acts, to score the lead roles in whatever lame play we end up spending our entire summer working on. Okay?"

"But what if—"

"Brie! Do Beyoncé or Christina or whichever lame MTV diva you're mostly admiring this week waste their time with what-ifs? No, they spend all their energy on looking fabulous and cutting down any bitch that dares get in their way. So, swear on the freakin' iPod."

"You are *so* gay."

"Finally you're on message about that, great. Have we got a pact or not?"

She pouted for precisely five seconds and then solemnly shook my hand. "Okay, we'll do this pact thing, then."

And then I made her get out the iPod that my mum's boyfriend, Merv the Swerve, brought us back from New York. We took an earbud apiece, and because it was Monday and I get to have it Monday, Wednesday, Friday, and alternate Sundays, I forced her to listen to the White Stripes all the way to Camden.